WISE LOVE

WISE LOVE

Jeanne McCann

iUniverse, Inc.
New York Lincoln Shanghai

Wise Love

Copyright © 2006 by Jeanne McCann

All rights reserved. No part of this book may be used or reproduced by any means, graphic, electronic, or mechanical, including photocopying, recording, taping or by any information storage retrieval system without the written permission of the publisher except in the case of brief quotations embodied in critical articles and reviews.

iUniverse books may be ordered through booksellers or by contacting:

iUniverse
2021 Pine Lake Road, Suite 100
Lincoln, NE 68512
www.iuniverse.com
1-800-Authors (1-800-288-4677)

ISBN-13: 978-0-595-39018-2 (pbk)
ISBN-13: 978-0-595-83409-9 (ebk)
ISBN-10: 0-595-39018-8 (pbk)
ISBN-10: 0-595-83409-4 (ebk)

Printed in the United States of America

To family, to friends, and to Ms. P, as always, who puts up with my time-consuming need to write.

Acknowledgements

Getting a story down on paper is the first part of the writing process and one of the easier steps. Getting someone to read and reread the story, turning it into a more cohesive work, is the hard part. Editors make all the difference in the world, turning a mediocre story into a well-crafted one. Thanks to Toni who is helping me to grow and learn more about the craft of writing.

Chapter 1

▼

"Alicia, can you tell me why you don't want to go to school?" Miranda O'Malley, child psychologist, watched the tiny little girl for any sign that she was listening to her. "Is someone bothering you at school?"

Miranda sat quietly in her chair as she watched Alicia closely. The small child's wavy blond hair curled sweetly around her tiny face. Her large, solemn eyes still refused to meet Miranda's as she fidgeted in the chair next to her. Alicia wore a pair of jeans and a bright green tee shirt, her tennis shoes tied with matching laces. She looked like a happy youngster, until someone took the time to look at her eyes, eyes exactly like those that Miranda saw over and over in her practice: old, fractured, and hurt. This pain was so deep that it was imbedded in the damaged child's heart and soul. Sometimes, similar eyes would look back at Miranda with a tiny kernel of hope or a glimmer of faith. These were the eyes of the children that Miranda helped to heal.

Alicia was one of these wounded children. She carried enormous hurt and pain inside her heart and it showed in her sad, blue eyes. Today she was refusing to do anything but kick at the chair leg. It was unlike Alicia to be so uncommunicative. She had been making great strides during her counseling sessions. Miranda sighed, slowed down her breathing, and tried to gently probe the young child's thoughts. Images flashed quickly into Miranda's mind, and she recognized the fear and anger that Alicia was hiding.

Their stepfather had sexually abused Alicia and her older sister, Tristan, for almost a year. A routine doctor's appointment had discovered the signs. Both of the young girls and their mother had been devastated. Overnight their home and lives had been destroyed along with their innocence. After the police were called in and their stepfather was arrested, the sisters and their mother had started therapy to help them heal from the horrendous tragedy. Miranda was working with both Alicia and her sister, and it was proving to be a painfully long process, especially since both girls had testified against their stepfather in court. He had been found guilty of multiple counts of sexual abuse and sent to jail for a term of ten years. The court case had taken almost two years from the time of his arrest until his ultimate incarceration. During those two years, both Alicia and Tristan had dealt with nightmares, stomachaches, and guilt. Their mother had been equally distraught, blaming herself for bringing a monster into their home and hurting her children. Now she found herself with no husband, no job, no money coming in, and two terribly damaged children. Even with the help of social services and Miranda's connections, nearly a full year passed before the small struggling family started to get back on track. The two young girls were still dealing with equal amounts of fear and anger; their mother carried guilt and horrible pain deep in her heart. Her guilt would remain for the rest of her life. Mothers were supposed to protect their children and she knew she had failed to do so.

Miranda knew that when an abuser is punished, their child-victims often feel enormous guilt, anger and loss. Miranda had dedicated her life and talents to healing these helpless victims. Every day she counseled innocent children who had been preyed upon by the adults that were supposed to protect them and keep them safe. Her practice had been set up years earlier to focus on these young victims. Miranda's graduation from college from the University of Washington had started her on the path. Working in the large city of Seattle, Washington, Miranda had built a network across the diverse city.

Sitting between the shores of Puget Sound and Lake Washington, the city of Seattle did an excellent job of providing social services to the ever-increasing population, the economy was strong, and the area was beautiful—filled with green forests and surrounded by mountains and water. Families gravitated to the area because of the many employment opportunities and recreational activities.

Where there were children, there would always be those who preyed upon them. These were the children Miranda had prepared herself to help. Her practice had started slowly, as she offered her skills to the social services department. She had been paid little and had been overworked, but she had loved the challenge. She knew she could make a difference in children's lives if she could help them overcome their suffering. Gradually, Miranda had gained a reputation for being successful with the most damaged of souls. After eight years of working within the social system, she had taken a leap of faith and opened her private practice. Every day she counted her blessings and gave thanks that her small practice was thriving and providing a service to the smallest in her community.

Miranda herself had had an almost idyllic childhood. She had been born and raised in the city of New Orleans, known for its diverse culture and acceptance of the unique or different. The environment was unique to the area and attracted an amazing collection of people all thriving in the warm, southern enclave. The city was full of history and supported the diverse talents that gravitated to the open, embracing culture. Along with Mardi Gras, the city celebrated music, good food, and artists of every caliber.

Miranda's family had been one of those set apart by their talents. Her grandmother, Rose, had been born with psychic abilities, as had her mother and Miranda herself. Due to their acceptance and guidance, Miranda felt comfortable and valued within her family. She grew up knowing that her psychic abilities could be put to good use, as any strong talent should be. It was people outside her family that had difficulties with a young child's ability to read their emotions. When her playmates' parents refused to allow Miranda to play with their children, Miranda's mother, Moira, would immediately speak to them explaining her daughter's unique and important talents, hoping that openness and honesty would positively influence their prejudice. To most New Orleaners, acceptance was unquestioned, and Miranda was rarely ostracized or picked on. Miranda's small circle of childhood friends didn't see anything odd about Miranda's ability to know exactly what they were thinking and feeling, and they accepted her, as she did them. None of her friends understood the real scope of Miranda's talents and that helped keep her childhood as normal as possible.

Many times over the years, Rose and Moira had used their psychic talents to assist the FBI and the police department in solving crimes. They both felt strongly that their gifts should be used to help others. They had instilled that sense of responsibility in their family, and Miranda grew up with the same desire to help those in need, especially children. Miranda had a natural affinity for helping the child least able to fend for herself. This commitment grew stronger throughout high school when she spent two summers working at a summer camp for abused and challenged children. The youngsters that attended the camp were so emotionally and physically damaged that they found it hard to interact with others. Bringing them together, along with dedicated counselors and teachers, was an attempt to help these children deal with all kinds of issues. Miranda had found it heartbreaking and life affirming. She had found her calling.

When she started college, she had gravitated toward psychology. Given her unique skills and talents, Miranda knew she could do good things for young children who ended up victims of abuse. She had uprooted herself after four years of college in New Orleans and moved to the University of Washington to complete her post-graduate work at the recommendation of her college counselor. Since she had been working in the field for many years now, her burning desire had not wavered. She was hoping Alicia and Tristan would eventually recover enough to get on with their young lives. She would do whatever was necessary to help them.

Even though their stepfather was locked up, both young girls still had terrifying nightmares that he would return to hurt them. Miranda knew what was bothering Alicia at that moment, and she needed to help the young girl admit her fears out loud. This would be an important part of her recovery.

"Alicia, your stepfather is going to be in jail for a very long time. He's never coming back to hurt you."

"But my mother loves him." Alicia's voice was low, but she was talking to Miranda and that counted for something.

"She loves you more, honey." Miranda placed her hand on top of Alicia's where it lay on the arm of the chair. "Your mother and I will make sure he's going to stay in jail for a *very* long time."

Alicia's sky blue eyes brimmed with tears. She looked up at Miranda, and Miranda squeezed the susceptible little girl's hand. "You promise?"

"I promise."

Miranda sensed the hesitation in Alicia's voice and tried to understand more of what was going on inside the little girl's mind. She sighed as she probed deeper, trying to help the vulnerable young child. "Alicia, there are lots of little girls that would want you as a friend. Have you met any new friends?"

"Yeah, Sandy and Beth."

"You met *two* girls?" Miranda knew that Alicia had pulled away from all of her friends during her ordeal, locking everything inside her damaged heart. She needed friends to love her unconditionally. Alicia and her sister attended middle school at Saint Bernadette's Catholic School. The school was doing everything it could to support the sisters.

Alicia looked up with interest at Miranda. "They take ballet."

Miranda smiled as she responded. "Don't you go to ballet?"

Alicia nodded her head and smiled up at Miranda. "I'm going to be in a class with them." Thanks to the kind-hearted generosity of an anonymous donor, both Alicia and her sister were able to resume their dance lessons, giving them some semblance of normality in their disrupted lives. It was one small step in the long journey toward health and security.

"Alicia, that's very good. Do you like these girls?"

Alicia bobbed her blond head up and down and smiled again. "They like me."

"What's not to like?" Miranda smiled and patted the little girl's hand. Miranda was pleased that Alicia was starting to interact with other girls her age instead of shutting down and avoiding connections with others. It was a healthy sign that Alicia was starting to talk about having friends. "You're one terrific little girl."

"Miranda, do you think they know?" Alicia ducked her head in shame.

This was what she'd been waiting to hear from Alicia. She had dealt with the same reaction in every child she saw overcoming abuse, the absolute shame around what had been done to them. Miranda's job was to make sure that her young clients knew that they had done absolutely nothing to be ashamed of. This was not an easy task.

"I don't think so, Alicia. But you know what? If your friends did find out, it would make them very sad that someone would hurt you and your sister. You did nothing wrong, Alicia. You're a very good little girl and it sounds like you have two wonderful new friends."

Alicia looked up to see the marvelous smile of the beautiful woman who always seemed to know what was bothering her. Alicia felt safe when she talked to Miranda. She liked the way Miranda always looked at her while she talked and always understood her. "Thanks, Miranda."

"You're very welcome, honey. Now, let's go return you to your mother and sister out in the lobby." Alicia took Miranda's hand and walked with her to the front office. Miranda nodded reassuringly to Mrs. Durham and handed Alicia off to her anxious mother. She and Alicia's sister were quietly reading together in the tastefully decorated room, full of comfortable chairs and couches. Children with whom Miranda had worked created the colorful artwork on the walls. It was important that the children entering her office felt at home in the space. "We'll see you both next week."

Miranda watched Alicia take one of her mother's hands and Tristan the other, as they headed down the hall to the elevator. The faint sound of humming drifted through the halls. Alicia hummed when she was happy. Miranda smiled as she turned back to her receptionist. It looked like Tristan and Alicia were two of the lucky ones who would be able to heal from a devastating trauma.

The children Miranda saw almost daily weren't always that lucky. She tried her very best with all of them, but some were so badly damaged they would never recover. These were the children that kept her awake at night. Miranda's heart broke over the fact that the most innocent were preyed upon. At times, it made her physically ill when she saw the horrible things that were done to children. She had pledged early in her life to focus her counseling skills on children, and day after day she worked with devastated parents and terrified youngsters. This took a serious toll on Miranda, but she was destined to do this work. Her heart told her it was right. If she helped just one child, her heartbreak was worth it.

"So how does tomorrow look?" Miranda asked her receptionist, Colleen Franks. Colleen always had a ready smile for everyone, and she favored Miranda with one now. Not only did she have the perfect personality for the job, she was extremely good at keeping a busy office running smoothly. She had mastered the art of filling out medical forms for insurance companies and was extremely well organized. She kept Miranda's thriving counseling office running smoothly, and Miranda would be lost without her. Her large smile and elfin face were appealing to both parents and children, and her easy personality calmed the most agitated client.

"Swamped—you're booked straight through 'til five."

"Great. What about Friday?"

"We have two appointments in the morning, three cancellations, and the afternoon is open. You were going to work on catching up on your files." Colleen couldn't prevent a grin from crossing her pretty face. Miranda might be a very talented and dedicated psychologist, but she was always behind in her paperwork. She was forever promising to catch up on her files and never seemed to manage doing it. It was a source of amusement between her and Colleen.

"I'm afraid an afternoon isn't going to make a dent in my paperwork." Miranda smiled. She knew her own failings well. "Why don't you get out of here and go see your husband and kids?"

"I was thinking about doing just that. Hey, how about coming over on Sunday for a barbeque? The weather should be good and you haven't seen what Will did with the back deck." Colleen and her family lived in a large rambler in Kent, a city southeast of Seattle. Miranda had been often to their home participating in many holidays and special family events. They had nearly finished remodeling both the interior and the exterior.

"I'd love to. What time and what can I bring?"

"Three o'clock and you don't need to bring a thing." Miranda enjoyed Colleen's family very much and she needed to have a relaxing day. She had been working non-stop for many weeks and was running out of energy.

Colleen had been Miranda's receptionist for almost ten years, and Miranda had not only watched her fall in love and get married to a very nice man, she had been in attendance when both of her sons were born. Colleen and her husband,

Will, were two of her closest friends. They were part of her small family. "You're not planning on setting me up with a blind date, are you?"

Colleen laughed at the look of utter horror on her boss's face. "No, we aren't planning to ambush you. Not that I've quit looking."

Colleen and her husband were forever trying to find someone to introduce to Miranda. They loved her to death and wanted to see her happily settled in a relationship. They kept their eyes open for the perfect partner for Miranda. Miranda hated to disappoint them, but she wasn't sure she would ever find someone to love. Or more specifically, that she would find someone who could accept her unique and special talents. Miranda needed that kind of acceptance from a life partner.

"I can find my own dates, thank you very much." Miranda sailed into her office, intent on cleaning up her desk and heading for home herself. She sighed as she saw the piles of files lying haphazardly on her desk, waiting for her attention. She might be a great psychologist, but she was horrible at her paperwork.

"So when are you going to go on one?" Colleen called as she pulled her coat on.

"One what?"

"You know what," Colleen laughed as she turned off her computer.

"Go home." Miranda had a grin on her face as she waved Colleen off.

Colleen chuckled again as she headed out the office door. "Goodnight."

"Goodnight," Miranda called as she sat down at her desk, which was completely buried with files. She really needed to get some of her reporting done. Sighing heavily, she stretched her back and made a decision. She was going home to take a nice hot bath and get into bed with a couple of the more urgent files. She just didn't have it in her to tackle the whole pile.

It had been a long day and Miranda needed to recharge her batteries. Helping children was her delight, but it took a lot out of her. Miranda didn't relish the fact that she didn't have someone to go home to. She was lonely a lot of the time.

She was a beautiful woman right down to her long, wavy hair, a blend of chestnut and red, with streaks of a lighter brown. She was a small woman, just like her mother and grandmother, standing five and a half feet tall. She was in excellent shape due to genetics, a healthy diet, and a busy life. She had the face of a woman much younger than her thirty-five years, and her large green eyes were as full of honesty as was her heart. It was her heart that kept her single, that and the psychic gifts that she had inherited from her mother, grandmother, and great grandmother. Her ability to read people's thoughts, especially if there were strong emotions involved, had destroyed her first real relationship in college. Subsequent relationships were weighed against her first broken heart, and many times Miranda walked away, unwilling to take a chance on getting hurt again. She would not be with a woman who didn't accept her for who and what she was.

Two hours later, Miranda sat quietly on the couch in her condominium, a glass of Merlot in her hand. The view of Puget Sound from her large picture window never failed to soothe her. From spring through the fall and winter months, the Sound changed colors, becoming at times green and fresh, brown and golden, gray and stark. The waters could be flat and glossy or whipped into a frenzy by the wind. The view was never boring, always beautiful, and always there. She loved her home and had taken great joy in decorating the space, filling it with a mishmash of artwork and elegant antique furniture. Her home, in the heart of the city, was in the unique area called Belltown. Belltown is a neighborhood full of families and single people who thrive on living downtown, close to everything Seattle has to offer. Within five blocks of her home Miranda could find live theater, art galleries, open markets full of fresh fruits, vegetables, flowers, and local art work. She could walk through the streets of the city among the giant skyscrapers, poke her head into the small businesses that populated the downtown corridor, or amble along the waterfront. She was active in her Belltown community and knew many of her neighbors on a first name basis. She should have been content and happy, but she wasn't. She was terribly lonely. She lay alone in bed at night aching for the intimate touch of another woman. Miranda needed passion in her life, and she had been unable to find it. This left a large hole in her heart.

Chapter 2

Mason Riley, a senior detective with the Seattle Police Department, slumped in her chair, her sharp blue eyes on the bulletin board across from her. Pinned to it were school pictures of two smiling children, adjacent to crime scene photographs of the same children lying naked, bloody and injured. Two kidnapped children, and absolutely no leads. One three-year-old boy, taken from his backyard where he'd been playing, had been left in Gasworks Park with evidence of torture and sexual abuse on his tiny body. He was so traumatized by his ordeal that he wasn't speaking to anyone. He'd been found two weeks after being taken, lying naked, his small body beaten beyond belief, and he hadn't uttered a word since.

Mason and her partner had been called to the scene as lead detectives, and she would never forget it. A jogger, who called in his grisly discovery, had found the boy. The first police officer on the scene had notified the medical team and the violent crimes squad. No matter how often Mason dealt with horror, she would never be immune to it. The first officer had been thorough and reported to Mason everything he had discovered while the medics had worked tirelessly on the tiny child. The surrounding area was a peaceful green space in north Seattle, and most days was filled with joggers, walkers, families, children, and pets. The view on a normal day was spectacular, but on that particular day, no one paid any attention to anything but the battered child. The horrible scene completely destroyed the friendly family atmosphere.

The young officer saw nothing but the victim. He had remained calm until he explained to Mason that a note had been literally pinned to the young boy's body, and then he began to cry, tears running unheeded down his usually stoic face. Mason's heart had broken for the young police officer whose heart was aching for the wounded child he'd found. He would have nightmares for a very long time.

Mason was painfully aware that police officers have extremely high rates of depression due to the things that they witness on a daily basis. They often deal with the worst of humanity and are not immune to feeling pain when they find an innocent who has been hurt. Even the most hardened of hearts could be broken at the sight of a badly hurt victim, especially a child. After witnessing so much ugliness during the course of a career, some officers turn to alcohol, some turn to drugs, and some abuse their spouses. A few seek counseling for help. Mason was going to make sure the young officer chose counseling. She had once been in the same position, and another senior officer had forced her into counseling. It was the best thing she had ever done. It had saved her sanity and her career. It had also made her pay attention to the officers around her, watching for burnout or other signs of trouble.

"Detective Riley, what kind of animal could do this?" he asked, as unashamed tears streamed down his cheeks.

"A sick one, officer. You did very well getting the medics here and preserving the scene. Your quick thinking will go a long way toward helping to catch the perpetrator."

"Will the little boy be okay?"

Mason could respond only with what she knew. "I'm hopeful that he will be, eventually. Now, you go back to the precinct and take a break."

"But I'm still on duty." The young officer was ashen, and Mason knew he was going to be dealing with what he had seen for a long time.

"That wasn't a request officer, that was an order." Mason's voice was quiet but firm.

"Yes, ma'am."

Just one week after the young boy had been found, the second child, a four-year-old girl, was taken from the playground of her daycare center. She had remained missing for almost two weeks before she was found in a parking lot in downtown Seattle. An observant Metro bus driver had discovered her in the lot that was almost completely empty of cars. The scene was dark with only streetlights for illumination. Within an hour the parking lot would normally be filled with all types of cars as employees arrived at work. It seemed almost surreal that a child could be abducted from the center that was dedicated to protect and nurture youngsters. The police who worked the scene recognized the irony. They spoke softly in the gloom while the paramedics worked on the victim before transporting her to the hospital. The young girl was bleeding profusely from the severe damage her small body had sustained. She remained in the hospital where medical personnel battled to repair her badly tortured body.

Her parents were angry and unbelieving that this could happen to their child. The girl was refusing not only to speak; she hadn't uttered a sound, nor even shed a tear when she saw her parents. It was as if her spirit had been snuffed completely out. Mason had been called to the scene immediately and had watched as the medics took care of the little girl. She vowed then and there that she would put the animal that committed these crimes behind bars. She would do everything in her power to find the crazy bastard who thought torturing a young girl was a game. Her partner was equally as dedicated and, between the two of them, they would find the perpetrator and lock him away for good.

"Jesus, Mason, I can't stand this case!" Matt swore as he stood waiting for the medics to load the little girl into the ambulance. His eyes were hard, his handsome face pale with anger and grim with resolve.

Mason found it difficult to speak, she was so sick to her stomach. Who could fathom the twisted mind that did things like this to a child? If she did one more thing in her career it would be to find the bastard. "Let's get to work and catch this fuck!"

Similarities in both crimes seemed to point to a single criminal, one very sick and depraved individual that preyed on young, defenseless children. Mason had been working for several years on major crimes, but this particular case was especially repulsive. She stared again at the bulletin board trying to see something—anything—that she hadn't seen before. The room was painted a ghastly shade of green; the long table at which she sat at was scarred with years of abuse, and the chair she sat in was sadly lacking in padding and back support. None of that counted. Everything of importance was pinned to the large corkboard covering the pockmarked wall. She had to find a break in the case before another child was hurt. She couldn't face the possibility that he or she might have already taken another victim. Her thoughts kept her awake at night and angry during the day.

The first child had been left with a note pinned to his naked back, and Mason picked up a photocopy and read it again. *"One little, two little, three little toys, four little, five little, six little toys, seven little, eight little, nine little toys, ten little perfect toys. Number one: are you ready to play my game?"* The bastard had plans for the future.

The second little girl had a note pinned to her thigh. *"One little, two little, three little toys, four little, five little, six little toys, seven little, eight little, nine little toys, ten little perfect toys. Number two: the game continues."* The notes were printed using a standard laser printer on plain white paper, the kind found in any office supply store. There were no fingerprints and absolutely no trace evidence. The perpetrator obviously had a plan, and Mason was hoping against hope to stop him before he could strike again.

The task force Mason headed was comprised of two FBI agents and six detectives, and they were at a dead end. No fingerprints were left on either child, no DNA was found, and there were no clues to follow. They could continue only to interview and re-interview everyone connected with the two children and their parents, in hopes of getting a lead, a connection, *anything* that might help them find the animal that thought hurting children was fun.

"Goddamn it!" Mason threw the file down on the table. She was so frustrated, and she feared it was just a matter of time before another child would be abducted.

"Hey, partner, what's up?"

Matt Gains pulled a chair out and straddled it backwards as he looked at Mason expectantly. They'd been partners for over three years and friends for almost eleven. Matt was a six-foot wall of muscle with short black hair and a broad smile. He was in every way a contrast to his five foot three, tiny, blond wife who was happily pregnant with their first child. Mason had been best woman at his wedding and loved his wife, Jena, just as much as she loved Matt. Jena was a funny, affectionate woman, and when she and Matt had met at a friend's home, he'd been completely smitten. Mason had listened for three weeks as Matt and Jena began to date. Matt had regaled her with stories about Jena. He had been equally as open with Jena about his partner and his best friend.

One evening when Matt and Mason had been stuck on the night shift, Jena had shown up at their dinner break with enough food for all three. She was charming, beautiful, and stood her own ground with Matt. She also went out of her way to win Mason's friendship, and she had succeeded. Mason spent many a night with the two of them, watching movies, drinking beer, and laughing. Jena had accepted Mason as a part of their small family. All three had no close living relatives, and they had bonded.

Matt had grown up in the foster care system, having been abandoned at a very young age by his mother. This made family even more important to him. Mason's parents had been older than most and by the time she was in her twenties both had passed away, her father from a heart attack and her mother from diabetes. Mason had no other cousins, or aunts and uncles that she knew about. The shocking death of Mason's brother while on a college-sponsored skiing trip had left her completely alone in the world. She had felt isolated and unconnected until she had met Matt. But Matt, Jena, and Mason were a family in the real sense of the word, loyal and loving.

The fact that Jena was currently on a mission to find Mason a girlfriend irritated the hell out of Mason. Jena wouldn't rest until Mason was happily involved in a relationship, and this terrified Mason. She had all but resigned herself to remaining single. But Mason couldn't stay mad at Jena. She knew Jena was matchmaking only because she loved her.

Mason expelled a deep breath, settled her mind, and tried to concentrate on the case. She and her team were missing something, something that would break the case open. She had to believe that or go crazy.

"We need to catch this freak before he hurts another child." Anger and frustration made her voice sharp.

Matt knew how she felt. He was equally as frustrated and angry. "We'll catch him."

Mason turned to look at Matt, her eyes red from exhaustion and stress. "This case is really getting to me."

"It's getting to me. I'm keeping Jena awake at night because I can't sleep." Matt nodded his head as he turned to look at the bulletin board. His large frame dwarfed the folding chair that he perched on. His eyes were locked onto the bulletin board.

"Hey Riley, Gains, anything new?" FBI agents Ben Lancer and Ann Johnson had joined the team after the first kidnapping. The two agents were dressed in their familiar dark suits, and their faces were as worn and drawn as Matt and Mason's. They were putting in as much time on the cases as Mason and Matt. They provided valuable access to all the tools and resources the FBI had to offer. It was rare that law enforcement agencies worked together without battles over jurisdiction; when it came to children, there were no turf wars. Everyone pitched in and did whatever was required. No one wanted these unspeakable crimes to continue.

"Nothing. We don't have a lead to follow up on. Neither child is speaking. Even hypnotizing them hasn't helped. They're too traumatized to speak. We have nothing, absolutely nothing."

"We've got the latest profile on this creep, nothing unexpected or unusual, though. It's probably a white male between twenty and forty years of age. He's driven by sexual gratification and sees the kids as nothing more than playthings. Our profiler believes that he's escalating and very possibly will kill a child if we don't catch him. It's all here in the full report."

"Thanks, Ben, I'll read it this evening." Ben Lancer placed the file on the table as he spoke. His voice was edgy with frustration. He wanted to catch the freak before he killed a child.

"Mason, I have a suggestion, and you can ignore it if you want, but we don't seem to have any other avenues. The FBI used this psychic to assist in solving the murder of a mobster's wife a year ago. The only witness was a very young child who refused to speak to anyone. He was in shock from seeing his mother killed right in front of him. This psychic specializes in young, traumatized children, and she was able to help us find the killer when we had no other leads. She somehow confirmed that the child had seen his father shoot his mother, and we were able to focus on him. He was eventually found guilty for the murder of his wife and sentenced to life imprisonment. This psychic has a great record. We wouldn't have been able to solve the case without her."

"A psychic! Jesus, Ben!" Mason had a hard time believing in things she couldn't see or feel. She thought that psychics and palm readers and the like were fakes who preyed upon gullible people. She had enough to do without resorting to weird, off the wall crap! Besides, she didn't have time to waste on worthless activities when a child was involved.

"I know it sounds odd, but the FBI uses them quite a bit. She's helped us with a few other cases that involved young children and has always been right on. I've never worked with her directly, but she comes highly recommended. I've got her information if you want to look at it."

"I don't know, Ben." Mason looked at him, her eyebrows raised in skepticism. Matt looked on in amusement; he wasn't quite so close-minded as his partner.

"What's it hurt? We don't have anything else to go with. What do we have to lose?" Ben would try anything to help them get closer to catching the perpetrator.

"Mason!" A detective interrupted their conversation with an urgent message. "A unit has just called in a report of a missing child in the Northgate area. She was taken from her bedroom within the last hour."

"Jesus, another one?" Mason's look was one of anger and sadness. "Come on, Matt."

"Mason, Ann and I will continue to go over the interviews we've got and look for connections. Call us if you need us." Ben was glad he wasn't going with them to the scene. He hated seeing what this type of crime did to the parents.

"Will do, Ben."

Matt and Mason headed silently for the door intent upon doing their jobs. Jena would say they had their cop looks on, serious and focused. Mason had no difficulty keeping up with Matt's long-legged stride, with her slender, athletic, five-foot-nine build.

Straight blond hair, that normally skimmed her shoulders, was held back in a ponytail to keep it out of her face. She was a pretty woman, her face all angles and high cheekbones, her blue eyes bright and usually filled with humor, her mouth full and sensuous. Anyone looking at her would comment on the well-toned body, as many a woman had done. Mason was a single, gay woman. She stayed in shape by working out religiously and paying attention to her diet. The men she worked with knew she was gay, and they teased her incessantly about her state of singleness, offering to find her a girlfriend. There was the occasional dyke comment, but usually not in front of Mason or any of the officers that worked with her. Her being gay had never been an issue with them, because Mason was a woman that men genuinely liked. And she was respected for her talent as a very hard working detective and as a fair team leader. She was someone everyone could count on.

Chapter 3

▼

The patrolwoman snapped to attention as Mason and Matt exited Mason's car and headed up the entry walk of a small, well cared for home in the Northgate area. Her uniform was spotless, her hat sat squarely on her head, and her stance was respectful. The two detectives passed her where she stood guarding the front of the home. It was a house for a young family, very appealing with its flowerbeds full of annuals and a large expanse of lawn. It was *not* a home that a child should have been taken from. The neighborhood abounded with houses surrounded by lush, green lawns. It had always been a family friendly area, close to parks, good schools, and a large shopping mall. It was an area of Seattle known for its quiet neighborhoods and older homes. Close to downtown for convenience, it should have been a very safe place for families and their children.

"Who's inside?" Matt asked, as he strode past the patrolman, his attitude completely businesslike.

"The first patrolman on the scene and the crime scene investigators are going over the bedroom. The detectives that caught the case are interviewing the parents in the living room."

"Thanks, officer." Mason didn't miss the smile or the look of interest on the young woman's face as she gazed at Mason. Mason had run into her at a party one evening, and the young woman had not been shy about exhibiting her interest in Mason. Mason had rebuffed her advances for several reasons: one, was she was way too young, and two, Mason never mixed business with pleasure—never. Mason liked to keep her job and her social life separate because she had found most women didn't understand her job or the horrifying things she had to deal with. And she had vowed never to be with another police officer. She had seen too many of those relationships go up in smoke due to the pressures of the job and the devastating things that cops dealt with. Additionally, Mason preferred not to share information about her job with people she met in a social situation. Given the fact that she worked all the time and refused to date other cops didn't give Mason many options for meeting anyone.

Mason climbed the front stairs and heard the heart wrenching sobs of the young child's mother. The crying was full of pain and shock, and Mason felt it grab at her heart. It was physically painful to listen to the young mother's anguish. She approached the couple as they sat huddled together on the couch. The small living room's decor included an entertainment center, a comfortable couch and two chairs. Toys strewn about on the carpet gave evidence of a child in residence. The sight of the young couple, pale with horror and disbelief, was all that Mason could focus on. The detective sitting across from them stood up as Mason and Matt approached. The other detective stood silently behind the couple. Both officials looked as devastated as the parents, but they were obviously struggling to maintain a professional demeanor.

"Mr. and Mrs. Andrews, these are Detectives Riley and Gains. They're the best detectives we've got when it comes to locating missing children. They'd like to ask you a few more questions, if you don't mind."

"Why aren't you out looking for my daughter? She's only two years old. We've already answered all your questions. Why can't you find her?" The young woman was hysterical as she burst into fresh, painful sobs while her equally distraught husband tried to console her. His face was ashen, his eyes red from crying. He turned to Matt and Mason and spoke softly.

"We'll do anything it takes to help find our daughter. Please, tell us what you need." His voice was rough with emotion. It was this quiet plea from the father that affected both Matt and Mason most deeply.

His look of utter sadness made Mason's stomach knot as she considered again what he and his wife were going through. No amount of talking could ever comfort a parent whose child had been taken.

"What's your daughter's name?"

"April. Here's a picture of her."

Mason and Matt looked down at the sweetest little face they'd ever seen. She was a pretty child, her cheeks rosy with health, her eyes glistening with humor, as she smiled engagingly at the camera. She was an appealing blond pixie. Mason had to close her eyes for a moment to control the rush of anger and emotion that made her want to scream in outrage.

"We want you to know that an Amber alert has gone out. This means all police, firemen, and emergency personnel are looking for April. The television stations are broadcasting every fifteen minutes, and so are all of the radio stations. A lot of people are looking for your daughter. We'll be working 'round the clock to locate her. Do you think you could answer a few more questions for me, while Detective Riley goes upstairs to talk with our team?"

Matt kept his voice low and pleasant as he spoke to the couple. They didn't need any more stress at that moment. Mason knew Matt was one of the best interviewers in the department. He would pull whatever information he could from the parents. Matt's patience and thoroughness made him a highly competent and well-respected detective.

Mason's talents lay in other areas, one of which was her ability to read a crime scene. While Matt spoke with the parents, she climbed the narrow stairway to the top floor and the child's bedroom and stood in the doorway, taking in the room. It was the room of a happy well cared for child, with sunny yellow walls, matching curtains, and bedspread. Her mind absorbed those facts as she tried to recreate what the monster had done this time. She knew it was the same man, her gut instincts told her it was, and she was praying that he had left some clue to his identity. She needed to find this little girl fast.

"Hey, Mason, you can come into the room. We've finished processing it."

"Hey, Jim."

Jim Weller was head of the criminal investigators' unit. After being a detective for fifteen years and taking countless night classes, Jim had become a crime scene investigator ten years earlier. He was now head of the unit, and he and his team were one of the best. He had volunteered his whole team for the missing children cases. The entire police department was on double duty as they tried to catch this crazy person before he hurt other children.

"What can you tell me? Tell me you got something that can catch this guy."

"Sorry, Mason. This guy knew what he was doing and came prepared. He came though the window by cutting the screen and the glass, then unfastening the latch. He climbed up a ladder that the husband says is usually leaning up against the garage. He staked this place out and knew exactly what he was doing. I would bet that he was already in the room when the child was brought upstairs after dinner. There's a little dirt and gravel over by the closet door and a few dirt smudges inside. If we get his shoe we may find the same small grit in his shoe tread. He also caught what looks like a nylon material on the window screen. I'd make a guess and say it was some kind of windbreaker at first look. We can match that, too, if we get the jacket. It's dark, navy blue, a fabric similar to what our police windbreakers are made of. The child's room is undisturbed otherwise, as far as her parents can tell. The mother said the little girl was playing with her toys on her bed while she and her husband were cleaning up after dinner. The father was coming up to read her a story when he discovered she was missing. That was a little over an hour ago." Jim delivered his information with calm deliberation, his hands in rubber gloves, his crime scene kit on the floor next to him as he waited for Mason's questions.

Mason's eyes tracked over the room and stopped at the bed where the child-size indent was still apparent on the bed next to some alphabet blocks and a teddy bear. Her heart clutched painfully in her chest as she realized that the young child was probably being abused at this very moment. She forced the thoughts away in order to concentrate.

"What about the ladder and outside? Any fingerprints showing up anywhere?"

"No prints that we can find. We'll take the ladder in with us. I think the perp wore gloves. We did find a couple of partial footprints underneath the last rung of the ladder. If you find the shoe, we can match. We took some casts and it looks like a standard athletic shoe; our guys think it's a Nike, but we'll have to confirm. We found lots of car tire tracks in the back, and we're assuming that's the direction he came and went in order to avoid being seen. Mason, this guy knows what he's doing. I think he knew this child; otherwise, there would be some sign of a struggle. She would have put up a fuss if a stranger had come in here. Her parents would have heard something. They say she was in the room for twenty to thirty minutes max. There's no sign of a struggle of any kind."

"Maybe he knew her, or more likely he just overwhelmed her too quickly for her to react. She's a small child. Were there any strange smells?"

"None that we could detect. Are you thinking chloroform?"

"Yes, but it leaves a distinctive odor. If this is a young male, as our profile suggests, he could have come out of the closet and snatched her so quickly she wouldn't have been able to do anything. Still, getting her out the window and down the ladder took some doing. If he knew her, he could have pretended it was a game and convinced her to go with him. We need to look carefully at the people close to this couple."

It was hard to do more than speculate on the profile due to lack of real, hard evidence. The FBI profilers had access to crimes all over the world and based their evaluations on historical predictors. Young males committed most crimes of this nature. It was extremely rare that a woman would commit such a crime.

"We're done here except for the guys doing the tire casting. They'll be here most of the night casting tire treads. If he parked out back, we'll find him. Mason, do you think it's the same guy?"

"I know it is, Jim. Thanks for processing so quickly."

"No thanks needed; just catch this freak."

Mason followed Jim and his crew down the stairs and signaled to Matt that she would be outside. Jim and his team loaded up all of their equipment and prepared to leave. The other crew would be working longer to get all the evidence from the back alley.

Contrary to what is often seen in popular television programs, the crime scene investigators that Mason worked with spent long hours in the lab running tests and looking for the one piece of evidence that might assist police detectives in solving a case. Mason had enormous respect for the division. She knew none of them would leave the scene without scavenging to find any piece of evidence that could identify the criminal. Many of Mason's cases had been solved by the exacting evaluation of crime scene evidence.

"Jim, call me when the reports are done and I'll come down to get them."

"Will do, Mason. We're going to stay the night until we get everything done. The FBI has volunteered to help us process the tire tracks so we can get finished as soon as possible. At least we might be able to identify *some* of the vehicles that passed though that alley. It may be a wild goose chase."

"I agree, but we have to look at everything. Thanks, I'll talk to you later."

Mason took a slow walk around the outside of the house attempting to discover exactly how the intruder had gotten in and was deep in thought and looking up at the house when Matt came out the front door and approached her.

"I think we've got as much as we can get from the parents tonight. Neither one is able to string a sentence together. If I have to, I'll come back tomorrow for some follow-up. We need to compare the information we got with the files we have on the other two children."

"You think it's him."

"Yeah, I do."

"The parents are terrified for their daughter. They're afraid it's the same guy that committed the other crimes. And they know what he did to those children."

The media had been all over this case from the beginning, and the terrible injuries that the children had been subjected to had been reported in the newspapers and on the local television stations.

"I doubt if they could give you anything meaningful right now. They asked me if it was the same guy, and I told them we didn't know. I hate lying to parents." Matt's face was tight with anger and sorrow.

"You didn't lie. We don't know for sure." Mason placed her hand on her partner's arm. "Goddamn it, Matt. It's him. I know it is! He's getting bolder with each child. He went into their home while the parents were right downstairs. He thinks he's invincible. I think Jim is right. This guy knows these kids. They aren't scared of him when he takes them. It's like he's a friend, and they just go with him."

"I agree with you, we need to go back over everything we have in the files from each abduction case. There has to be some contact in common. We've missed something somewhere. There's a connection." Matt's face displayed frustration and anger.

"Did you get anything from the parents that we might follow up on?"

"Nothing that stands out; I want to get everything into the database and go over it all again along with the first patrolman's notes from the scene, just to be sure. I'll have to come back and talk to them again, but we have enough to get started."

Given the fact that there was clear evidence of a break-in, and the strong probability that the same person had done all three kidnappings, the parents were not high on their suspect list. They would let the first officer on the scene investigate the parents. Matt and Mason would continue looking for connections to the other children.

"A patrol unit is going to stay outside the parents' home for the night, and we have two detectives that will stay the night just in case there's any contact from the perp."

"Good. And the husband's parents are on their way over. Christ, Mason, I hated the way that woman looked at me." Matt ran his fingers through his short hair, sadness in his voice. He couldn't help but think about his pregnant wife and his own child. It would kill him if someone took his child. He could imagine what the young parents were going through.

"I know. Come on, let's get back to the station."

"Okay. Hey, Mason! Did you notice how that patrolwoman was checking you out?" Matt asked with a grin as they headed back to the car. It seemed incongruous that Matt could tease Mason right in the middle of such a serious case, but it was one way they both had to alleviate stress. Besides, Matt would never pass up any opportunity to harass Mason.

"Give me a break, Matt." Mason rolled her eyes as she climbed into her car. "She's way too young."

"I can see that she's attracted to old ladies. She would have to help you to your car if you went out on a date," Matt teased, as he flashed his trademark dimples at Mason.

"Bite me! I'm not that old," Mason responded as she began to drive back to the stationhouse. "I just want to date someone that was alive when I was in high school."

"Mason, you're never going to meet anyone if you don't date people you run into at work."

"*You* did. Besides, you know my rules."

"Jena met someone at work she wants you to meet."

"Matt," Mason growled. "I can find my own dates."

"In this lifetime?"

"Cut it out."

Chapter 4

Mason and Matt were striding down the hall to their desks when one of the detectives called to Mason. "Mason, the Chief wants to see you."

"Thanks, Sela, I'm on my way."

Mason gathered her papers together and headed down the hall to the Chief of Detective's corner office. She was not looking forward to the discussion. She didn't have anything new to report. The Chief was not going to be pleased with the way the case was going. He had asked Mason to keep him up to date on the case, and he wanted it solved quickly.

"Mason, have a seat." The office was a step up from the detective bullpen, but not a big step. It wasn't larger than ten by ten and was dominated by a large desk and the even larger figure of the Chief of Detectives.

"Thanks, Chief."

"Give me a status in twenty minutes or less. I have to update the Police Chief in an hour in his office."

"We've been going over all the interviews from all three sets of parents and nothing is standing out. We're going to be finishing up all the lab work on the footprint and the tire casts overnight, but nothing has popped from that so far. An Amber alert was issued. Chief, we don't have any leads to follow. This guy knows what he's doing forensically. He hasn't left anything for us to use to find him with."

"You think this latest abduction is him?"

"I know it's him."

"Goddamn it, she's a two-year-old girl!" He jerked out of his chair and ran his hands through his grey hair. He stood a healthy six-one, but years behind the desk had added extra girth around his middle. His suit was well cut but did nothing to mask his strength and stature. He was a man who had come up through the ranks.

"April, her name is April." Mason always knew the names of the victims in her cases; it was her way of honoring them.

"Find this guy. I want everyone helping on this. Someone has to have seen something." The Chief's voice rose and his face reddened with irritation.

Chief Marston, Art to those who knew him, was a fair and hardworking Chief of Detectives. He expected his detectives to do their jobs and to do them well. If they needed anything, he would get it, if possible, as long as his workers were putting out the effort. On the other hand, those who slacked off on his watch were guaranteed a demotion or transfer. Mason liked Art very much and had learned a lot from him. He had a keen mind and twenty years of detective work for experience. He would get actively involved in cases that were politically sensitive in order to reduce the pressure on his detectives. Right now, he was as frustrated as his lead detectives. He was dealing with an escalating situation with the media as well. If this criminal wasn't caught soon, the public would panic and a huge public relations nightmare would be in full swing.

"I'll let you know if we get anything today. The FBI is running all the tire tracks for us."

"How has it been working with them?"

"Good; they've been providing a lot of support, and both agents are putting in as much time as our team."

"Do you need anything?"

"I might be bringing in a child psychologist to talk to the first two children. She has some talent in understanding children who have been traumatized." Mason skipped over the fact that the woman was also a psychic. She would deal with that fact later, if she actually decided to ask her for assistance. She still wasn't totally convinced that she wanted to involve her, but she had nothing else to go on. She was getting desperate.

"Let me know what the cost is. I'll need to cover it from somewhere else in the budget."

"Will do, Chief."

"Mason, how long have you been without sleep?"

"Not too long."

"I don't want my favorite detective burning out. Go get some sleep. You're doing a good job, but you can't keep up this pace." Chief Marston hadn't missed the dark circles under Mason's eyes. He also knew how much time she and her team were putting in on the case.

"I'll get some sleep."

"Good, now get out." He barked at her as he sat heavily back in his chair.

Mason smiled at the Chief and left his office. She appreciated his no-nonsense approach and his support of his detectives. Mason dropped her files on top of her desk and headed down the stairs to the labs. She needed to check on the progress of processing the evidence. She was hoping that the lab had found something—anything—that she could use.

"Hey, guys, how's it going?" Mason asked, as she entered the pristine lab office. In direct contrast to the rest of the building, the forensics unit was high tech spotless, and meticulously organized. The department was in the basement of the police precinct house and housed a large staff of scientists and technicians.

"Great, now that you're here. A good looking woman makes it all worthwhile."

"Ron, don't you have anything better to do than harass Mason?"

Mason ignored the taunt and turned to Jim Weller who was sitting at his desk compiling his report. She was used to Ron Walker's comments. He made one every time Mason entered the lab, and no number of threats could cool him off. Mason had chosen to ignore him over shooting him. "Where are we, Jim?"

"We've got a good footprint, and it's a Nike running shoe, one that's sold just about anywhere you can buy shoes. If you catch him with it on, we can match it. It has some distinctive wear patterns. Based on the size of the print and the depth, we can estimate that he's probably a good one-eighty to two hundred pounds. The length between footprints makes us think that he's six feet, maybe a little taller. The threads we found on the screen are nylon, consistent with a navy windbreaker-style jacket. You know, like our police windbreakers. The tire prints aren't giving us anything. Every type of print is in that alley, and we need a suspect's car to check them against. We have over one hundred at last count. The fine gravel we found in the room is consistent with the kind used on baseball fields and in some gardens for drainage. We might be able to match it if you get a shoe with the same stuff in the tread."

"No fingerprints on the ladder?"

"None so far."

"Great job, Jim."

"I'm sorry we don't have more for you to go on." Jim looked tired, his eyes red-rimmed with exhaustion.

"Maybe you ought to go home and get some sleep. You must be beat."

"I'll go home when you go home."

"I'm going to go home in a bit."

"Good, I'll have our written report on your desk in the morning."

"Thanks, Jim, I appreciate that."

Mason walked slowly back upstairs, her feet dragging as she headed for her desk and the files that were piled high on top of it. The paperwork was never ending, and it could be overwhelming at times. "I thought you were going home, Mason."

"Hey, Ben, I'm going right now. What about you?"

"I'm out of here. I just wanted to see if you had thought any more about bringing that psychic in."

"I have thought about it, and I'm desperate enough to give her a try."

"Why don't I have her come in and you can talk to her? See what you think?"

"Can you get her in early tomorrow morning?"

"I'll call her right now and see if I can get her here by seven."

"Good. If we decide to use her services, I want to get started on setting up an interview with each of the victims. This latest little girl will have been missing for twelve hours and we're running out of time."

"I'll get her here. How early are you coming in?"

"I'll be here by six, so anytime after that will do."

"Good. If it works out, I'll have a unit pick her up in the morning and bring her here."

"Ben, go get some sleep."

"I'm gone. You do the same."

Mason trotted down the stairs to the parking garage and climbed into her car. She was beyond tired and wanted to go home and drop into bed face first. She hadn't been getting more than five hours of sleep since this case started.

Mason's apartment was in Ballard, one she'd been living in for a long time. It was in a secluded area of Seattle, close to the Sound, and known for its Scandinavian roots. Mason liked the small downtown, and her apartment was within running distance of the beach. She liked to run along the waterfront as much as possible. It helped her to turn her mind off and tune out the horrors of her job. Mason enjoyed living in the area. She actually had enough money saved to buy a house, but every time she started the process she got cold feet. She always thought that she would have a partner by her age, and together they would buy a house. She was comfortable with her two-bedroom apartment and it was a short twenty-minute drive to work on a good day. Besides, it was in a safe neighborhood and easy for her to take care of.

Mason fixed a light snack for dinner, did a quick workout, read her mail, and took a short, hot shower. It was almost eight o'clock before she crawled under the covers of her bed. She lay quietly trying to turn her mind off long enough to get some sleep. Mason's apartment was homey. She had gradually filled it with furniture and artwork that was traditional and cozy. But she spent very little time there; it made her sad to sit in her apartment alone. Mason missed the companionship of another woman. To combat her loneliness, Mason biked, hiked, and did everything she could to keep herself busy. The mild climate in Seattle and the bike paths around the city provided Mason with lots of areas to explore.

She had been a solitary person since childhood partly because she was so much younger than her brother. Their parents had almost given up on having children when they had Mason's older brother, Alex, who was seven years older than Mason. They had a small house just north of the Greenwood area, close to the University of Washington. Mason and Alex hadn't been all that close growing up, and Alex had been a troubled young man. He had several brushes with the law due to heavy drinking while in high school. Mason on the other hand, found school challenging and worked hard to excel. She was also a natural athlete which gave her an outlet for her boundless energy. Mason's parents didn't understand either child and were distant and unaffectionate. Mason hadn't gone without material things while she was growing up, but she had always felt she was lacking something. When her parents had passed away, she had grieved quietly and finished high school on her own, intent on attending college.

Miraculously, Alex had made it to junior college at Seattle Community and had started partying in earnest. Even though Mason had known he was playing around with drugs, she had been devastated when he overdosed. She could still remember the telephone call.

"Mason Riley, this is Officer Saunders from the Seattle Police Department. Your brother, Alex Riley, has been taken to Harborview Hospital where he's being treated for a drug overdose. Would you like us to send a police car to bring you to the hospital?"

"No, uh, I can drive."

"Is there someone who can come with you?"

"No, our parents are dead." Mason had no one, not even a best friend to call. She had friends in high school but no one she was close to. "I'll leave right now."

Mason's life had been thrown into a tailspin. At eighteen years old, she had to bury her brother and take care of all the financial arrangements. She had cried herself to sleep for weeks, scared, alone, and lost. Even though she and Alex weren't close, she missed having a brother, and the house they grew up in was empty. Not long after Alex's death, she sold the house to rid herself of painful memories. Those feelings had persisted for almost a year into her college career at Seattle University.

It was at the start of her sophomore year that Mason had met a twenty-two year old assistant professor named Marni Olson. A playful and outrageous lesbian, Marni had pursued Mason with a vengeance, recognizing a kindred spirit. Mason had always known she was attracted to women but had never acted upon this attraction. Marni had awakened the slumbering passion buried deep in Mason's carefully guarded heart. Mason had fallen hard, and for over eight months lived on sex and affection, her loneliness gone. But Marni was too busy to settle down with just one woman. Predictably, Mason's heart had been shattered, and once again she was alone and terribly sad.

Mason's college years were filled with brief affairs with women lasting long enough to assuage her loneliness. Her main focus was getting through college with a criminology degree. Mason had a goal to become a police officer and arrest every drug dealer in existence. She may not have been able to prevent her brother from destroying himself with drugs but she could help others by getting drugs off the street. It became almost an obsession with Mason, one she shared with no one else until she met Matt.

Mason had been attending the police academy for almost a month in a class of twenty-six cadets. Matt was another cadet in the class, quiet and gorgeous looking, and Mason had made the assumption that he was conceited and arrogant. She had been dead wrong. Studying for a test, Mason had holed up in the library by herself; she was going to ace the test.

"Hey, Mason." Ben stood grinning next to the table where Mason was sitting.

"Hey, Ben."

"Do you want to study together? I'm worried about this test."

Mason looked up into Ben's eyes and saw nothing but friendliness. She made a quick decision, one for which she would be grateful for the rest of her life. "Sure, why not?"

From that day on, Matt and Mason had become friends and were almost inseparable. Matt had become the brother that Mason wanted in her life, and Mason had become Matt's family. They had studied together, worked out together, and graduated from the academy with honors together. Luck had not been with them after graduation when they were assigned to different precincts, but that hadn't altered their friendship. They made time for each other, and the friendship had grown in strength and love.

"Mason, why don't you date?" Matt had asked one evening as they sat at a local bar drinking a beer.

Mason sighed before answering Matt. She was afraid he wouldn't remain her friend after she told him she was gay. She had been wrong. "I'm a lesbian, Matt."

"Hell, I know that, but you never go out with anyone. Do you need me to find you a woman?"

Mason choked on her beer. "You—find *me* a girlfriend?"

Matt grinned back at her surprise. "Yeah, you aren't doing a very good job of it."

"I don't see you doing much dating."

"I'm holding out for the perfect woman."

"Well, so am I." Mason grinned back at him.

"Life's a bitch!"

"Yes, it is!"

Mason sighed deeply as she lay in bed. She knew she was lucky to have Matt and Jena. She loved them dearly, but there was emptiness inside her. She wanted a lover, a partner, and passion—she needed passion in her life. Mason slid slowly into sleep, her heart troubled, her mind still permeated with thoughts of her work.

Chapter 5

▼

Mason slept heavily until five the following morning when her alarm rang shrilly. She dragged herself into the shower and was dressed and out the door by five-thirty. Mason had lots of practice getting dressed quickly, and by now it was second nature. She donned her usual slacks and matching jacket, harvest gold in color. Her fellow detectives teased her about her fashion sense and fastidiousness, especially since she wore a shoulder harness over her silk shirt, her cell phone and her gold badge on her belt. Mason's one vice was her need to wear stylish clothes despite the fact that her job could be hard on them. She liked dressing up. She pulled out of her apartment parking lot and drove quickly to work, a cup of coffee in her hand, her mind focused on the day ahead. Many days Mason admired the view of Puget Sound to her right as she made the quick trip to work. Some days it was a source of delight, but today was not one of those days.

She was at her desk reading the completed crime scene files when Matt flopped into the chair next to her. "Hey, partner, how's Jena feeling?"

"Great, the baby was kicking all last night. She's feeling good, and the baby is healthy. I can't believe she's due to deliver in a few weeks." Matt's face showed consummate pleasure at the prospect of becoming a parent. He and his wife were ecstatic about the upcoming event, and Mason was just as excited for the two of them. She brought a new present for the baby every time she went over to visit.

Shortly after Matt and Jena had learned of their impending parenthood, they had purchased a home on the eastside of Seattle in Kirkland. It made a long commute for Ben, but Jena's job at a small software startup company kept her in Kirkland. It was a nice area in which to raise a family. Mason was envious of the happiness they had found with each other. She yearned for happiness and a relationship of her own.

"Yep, and then you'll be inundating me with stories about how smart and cute your baby is. Let's just hope she looks like Jena and not her dad." Mason always teased Matt about his looks. He was a man that could best be described as beautiful. His good looks made him the brunt of a lot of ribbing from cops and criminals alike. When Mason had first met Matt, she thought he would be self-absorbed with his gorgeous looks. But he wasn't. His looks made him shy and uncomfortable and that endeared him to Mason. He was a genuinely nice man, caring, and generous. And as Mason was fond of saying to him, you can't help it if you're born beautiful. Matt would blush with embarrassment at her comment. But he gave as good as he got in the teasing department.

"Hey, you're looking mighty fine this morning. Do you have a date tonight?"

"Shut up," Mason responded with a grin and a shake of her head.

"Matt, I'm glad Jena is feeling so good." Mason smiled up at her friend and partner. Especially during the worst cases, she was glad Matt was by her side.

"Pretty soon, you're going to be an aunt." Matt grinned as he loped over to his desk not five feet away from hers. He sat down on the rickety wooden chair and flipped the switch on his battered computer. There were ten desks in the room housing the detective bureau, all old and marked with the abuses of time. Money was not spent on furniture and computers, but work went on. The nine detectives that shared the space grumbled and then worked long hours, committed to solving every crime that passed their desks.

Mason felt a rush of emotion and affection as she watched him settle in his chair. She loved Matt and Jena more than anyone else, and she was looking forward to spoiling their first child. They were her family in every sense of the word. She spent every holiday with them at their home.

"So where are we on this miserable case?"

"Let's review the information we've got. We know this guy leaves no prints or evidence, so he has knowledge of forensics. He wears a navy blue nylon jacket of some sort. He was wearing Nike running shoes during the last abduction. His height is around six feet and his weight one eighty-five to two hundred. They found coarse sand in the girl's room that wasn't from the yard. It's either from a ball park or a garden." Mason recited as she read from the CSI crime report. They had collected a lot of evidence from the last crime scene.

"He took the first boy from the child's own backyard, the second child from her daycare playground, and this last one from her bedroom, while her parents were one floor below."

"He tortured and sexually abused both of the first two children before leaving them naked, somewhere where they would eventually be found, notes pinned to both of them. He sees them as objects to play his game with, and he wants us to play with him. He's very good at this, which makes me think he's done this before, and he's escalating. If we don't catch him soon, he's going to kill a child. He kept the first one for two weeks before dumping him, and he kidnapped the second child a day after he got rid of the first one. We're on the second day after the kidnapping of April, our third child. We need to find her quickly."

"So what's our plan?" Matt asked his partner, his faith in her absolute.

"We need to get the FBI to run his modus operandi through every single database at their disposal. He has to have done this before. We might get lucky and be able to identify him from similar crimes. Meanwhile, we go back through every single note we have on all the parents' interviews. We need to know what they were doing before the children were kidnapped. There has to be some connection with each child he has taken."

"I'm on it right now."

Mason smiled as Matt got up and headed for the conference room. She couldn't ask for a better partner and friend. While Matt and his team reviewed all their interview notes in the conference room, pulling out every bit of information that might link the cases together, Mason again read the FBI profiler's report on their kidnapper. The report didn't tell her anything she didn't already know. He had probably done this before and was an organized, methodical predator.

"Mason, the woman psychologist agreed to come in and talk with you. She'll be in here in about thirty minutes and she doesn't expect payment for her services."

"Thanks, Ben. I'll be in the small conference room going over the forensic reports."

"I'll bring her in when she gets here."

Mason sat back in thought. It was interesting that the woman would drop everything to volunteer her services at no charge. Couldn't she use her skills to make lots of money? It seemed to Mason that there were thousands of people who would pay a purported psychic for information about their dead relatives and loved ones and to foretell the future.

Chapter 6

Miranda hastily finished dressing and pinning her hair up, called Colleen and asked her to reschedule her morning appointments. She understood the urgency conveyed by the FBI agent, and she would do anything to help find the missing little girl. She grabbed her briefcase and hurried downstairs to meet a police unit in front of her building. She was unsure as to exactly what might be expected of her, but she had worked for the FBI before, and her mother and grandmother had helped many police departments over the years. The women in Miranda's family believed that the gifts they had should be used for good. Though she had been met with skepticism and occasionally downright rudeness, she had not shied away when asked to help the police and the FBI.

She swung through the entrance doors as a police car slid to a stop in front of her building. A young police officer stepped out of the car and approached her. His uniform was pressed with sharp creases and his badge shone. He looked professional and friendly. "Miranda O'Malley, I'm Douglas Kent, and I'm going to take you back to the downtown precinct."

"Good morning, Officer Kent. Thanks for picking me up."

"No problem."

The officer opened the front passenger door for her.

"It's pretty early, Officer. Are you just starting work?"

"No ma'am, I'm just ending my shift. I get off at seven."

"You worked all night?"

"From eleven on."

"I don't think I could get used to working nights."

"It's not too bad."

The young officer and Miranda chatted during the short drive to the police precinct. The city was silent and empty at the early morning hour, but when the work day started the streets would fill up with cars and busses as thousands headed to their jobs. The downtown area was filled with towering office buildings that housed the many businesses supporting the thriving city. The sidewalks would be filled with people moving from building to building in a steady stream. Miranda loved to walk through downtown Seattle and watch the people. The area attracted people who enjoyed the outdoors and many could be seen jogging and walking the city streets. It almost looked like a different city when the streets were empty and dark. She gazed up at the darkened skyscrapers as they headed down Third Avenue toward the police precinct.

The officer pulled the car into the parking garage under the building and led the way into the elevator. They rode up to the main lobby and exited.

"Here you go, ma'am. I need to call upstairs and let them know you're here."

"Thank you, Officer."

Miranda was escorted into the quiet, nearly deserted precinct lobby. There were a few officers near the front desk talking quietly, but not much more was happening, which surprised Miranda. She would have thought there would be a lot of activity at the large police station. Officer Kent went to the desk and dialed the telephone as she glanced around. A large, tall desk with room for four uniformed police officers behind it dominated the lobby. Several telephones rested on the desk. Miranda could see into the open door behind the officers to a large room where several uniformed officers sat at desks or stood around talking. The rest of the lobby was completely empty and a little dingy, with wooden benches and chairs placed randomly around it. The lobby smelled of coffee, aftershave lotion, and, of all things, pizza. Mason looked back at Officer Kent and, after a brief conversation, he hung up the telephone and turned to smile at Miranda.

"They're sending someone downstairs to escort you up to the conference room."

Miranda stood quietly next to the young man and continued taking in her surroundings. While Miranda looked around, she was unaware of the young police officer's scrutiny. He couldn't help admiring a beautiful woman. Her dark brown hair was gathered into a loose bundle of curls at the back of her head. He took in the forest green skirt and matching suit jacket that showed off her excellent legs and figure. She stood about five and a half feet in her high heels and had the most appealing face he'd seen in a long time. She had large green eyes that sparkled and her cheekbones were high, but it was her mouth that he kept staring at. Full, luscious lips and straight white teeth made her smile absolutely stunning.

She was extremely sexy looking, and he couldn't keep from staring. He noticed the other officers were also making their own observations.

"Miranda O'Malley, my name is Agent Lancer, Ben Lancer."

"It's nice to meet you, Agent Lancer." Miranda looked at the tall, slender man dressed in a dark suit and shook his extended hand in greeting.

"Call me Ben, please. Follow me and we'll go right up to the conference room so I can introduce you to the detective in charge of the case. She'll review it with you."

Miranda followed the tall man up the stairs and down a corridor. The stairwell walls were scuffed, and the hallway was dimly lit. The floor sported grimy linoleum. They passed through a roomful of desks covered with computers and tall piles of paper. There were a couple of men speaking together at one desk, but the rest of the room was devoid of people. Ben entered another doorway into what appeared to be a small conference room. Miranda entered behind him and stepped to the side so she could see the other person in the room. She felt a jolt as she looked into the blue eyes of a beautiful blond seated at the table across from where she stood. They locked eyes, and Miranda tried not to reveal what she was feeling. The woman held the stare as she looked back at Miranda.

"Detective Mason Riley, this is Miranda O'Malley."

"Hello, Detective Riley." Miranda shook the outstretched hand of the detective and experienced a series of flashes that shot through her mind. It shook her considerably, but she revealed nothing to the woman who watched her so intently. Her mind was bombarded with thoughts and feelings so strong she had to shield herself quickly.

Mason felt a surge of energy when she shook the woman's hand, and she almost said something about it. She'd never experienced anything like this before. It was as if someone had infused her with power. She was also surprised at how utterly beautiful she was and how professional looking. Somehow, Mason had thought the woman would look more stereotypically psychic, wearing a loose-flowing dress and heavily draped with beads.

"Ms. O'Malley, please have a seat."

Miranda sat down across from the woman detective and Agent Lancer sat beside her. The seat was a stiff wooden chair, but Miranda's mind was so engaged that she scarcely noticed. Ben remained silent as he waited for Mason to begin her questions. This was Mason's show. Miranda placed her briefcase on the floor next to her chair, her eyes never once leaving Mason's face. She, too, waited for the woman to speak.

"I know Agent Lancer has given you some background about this case, but before we go any further I'd like to get an idea of what type of psychic abilities you have."

Miranda answered with deliberate slowness. "I can read strong emotions like fear, excitement, anger, and happiness, if I open myself up to someone."

"You can read a person's feelings?"

Miranda didn't have to be told Mason didn't believe in psychics. Her expression and body language gave her away, not to mention the waves of complete disbelief emanating from the detective.

"In a way, I open myself up, and I see flashes of their thoughts, their experiences, and their feelings, particularly if they've gone through something traumatic."

"Ben told me you're a child psychologist and use your skills in your work. Why do you work with just children?"

Miranda smiled at the woman who had yet to stop staring at her.

"Children are more open with their feelings and thoughts. When they've been emotionally or physically damaged, many times they can't articulate their anger and fear. If I can understand what is scaring them, I can help them overcome it and heal."

"Does your talent work only with children?"

"Detective Riley, would you like a demonstration?" Miranda smiled good-naturedly at the skeptical woman.

"If you could?" Mason was prepared to be disappointed.

Miranda took a slow, deep breath and relaxed, focusing on Mason's face. She was silent for just a moment before speaking. "I can assure you I'm not a whack job."

Mason had the good grace to flush with embarrassment as she realized what Miranda had just read from her mind. When Miranda grinned at her, Mason felt her body react with unexpected attraction to the compelling woman.

"I don't think I will say *those* thoughts out loud." Miranda smiled as she watched Mason's face darken further with embarrassment. Mason had been thinking about what it might be like to make love with Miranda, and she was sure Miranda had gotten a glimpse of her thoughts. She refocused her attention on the case and the missing girl.

Miranda sighed, reached out and covered Mason's hand where it lay flat on the desk. "You will find April and you will catch the man who is doing this. She will be okay."

Mason stared back at Miranda, feeling her probe her thoughts and feelings. Somehow, it didn't surprise her nor did she have the feeling of being invaded. She felt like she already knew her.

"Ms. O'Malley, I need to know if you could interview the first two victims and see if you can help them articulate who and what they saw. Neither child is speaking to anyone right now. They've been terrified into silence. One thing I do want to make perfectly clear: the children come first, and if I feel that anything we're doing will harm them in any way, I'll stop it."

Miranda's hand still rested on top of Mason's and she felt the connection all the way to her toes. Sighing softly, Miranda smiled up at Mason. "I wouldn't do anything to harm a child, ever. I can help these children by alleviating some of their fears, but I can't guarantee that they'll articulate something that will prove to be of value, or that I can read everything that happened to them. But I will at least try to help these poor children rest easier. I'll help any way I can."

"Good."

Mason stood up pulling her hand from under Miranda's and smiled down at her. "I'll go get the files I have on the children and the case. I'll have to wait a couple of hours before calling the parents to set up a time for you to speak to the children. If you don't mind, for now I don't want to tell them you're a psychic."

"I don't mind. One thing you need to know is I don't probe people's minds or thoughts without permission, unless it's a child in need of my help. It goes against everything I value to trespass on another's feelings. I'll not do anything I think is wrong."

"Fair enough, I'll go get the files. Ben, do you want to get Matt's information?"

Ben had remained silent the whole time, watching the dynamics between the two women. It was something to watch. He wasn't quite sure exactly what had happened between the two women, but something had.

Ben and Mason left the room, and Miranda slumped in her chair. She'd seen far more in her connection with Mason than she bargained for. She hadn't been expecting anything close to what she now knew. From the disjointed images she'd seen, she had been able to recognize one thing for sure. She knew they would be lovers. She didn't know when, but she knew they would be. She also knew that there would come a time when Mason would have to make a decision about whether to trust Miranda and her psychic abilities. And Miranda didn't know whether she would. She'd had an unusually strong connection with Mason, one she'd never experienced before with an adult. It terrified her.

Ben carried the pile of files in to Miranda and laid them on the table in front of her.

"Here you go. Can I get you some coffee, tea, water?"

"I'd love a glass of water, if you don't mind."

"No problem. Mason said for you to review all this information, and then we'll answer any questions you have."

"Thank you, Ben."

Miranda reached down into her briefcase and pulled out a pad and pencil. Arranging them on the table next to her, she picked up the first folder. Miranda had a lot of reading and preliminary work to do before she applied her abilities. She wanted to know as much as possible about what had happened to the children before she saw them in person. She'd need to prepare herself extensively in order to help them. The small, claustrophobic room with the conference table and wooden chairs were forgotten as Miranda concentrated on the files in front of her.

An hour and a half later, Miranda finished writing the last few questions on her tablet and stretched luxuriously, her back protesting against the uncomfortable chair.

Mason had been surreptitiously watching her for several minutes from the doorway, fascinated with her and unwilling to disturb her. Miranda had known the minute she stepped up behind her. She'd felt Mason's energy radiate from her in waves. Miranda could have spoken to her without turning around but she remained silent, waiting for Mason to speak first. Somehow she and Mason had a very strong connection, and Miranda didn't question it. She knew that Mason was meant to come into her life. Her heart had recognized her.

"Have you finished reading the files?"

"Yes. Can I ask you something?"

"Sure." Mason came into the room and stood next to Miranda. She was surprised to see Miranda's large green eyes filled with tears. It softened her attitude immediately. Miranda was a woman who grieved when children were wounded.

"How do you deal with these kinds of cases involving such horrible things happening to children? Doesn't it break your heart?" Miranda's voice was soft, her eyes full of compassion.

Mason took the time to collect her thoughts before she responded. It was hard for Mason to share her innermost feelings.

"It does break my heart, and some cops deal with it by drinking, others by getting angry and taking it out on their families."

"How do *you* cope?" Miranda's eyes stayed locked on Mason's face as she waited for her response.

"I solve their cases, and if I have a really tough one, I work out until I'm completely exhausted and can't think about it. It's important that I remain focused on catching freaks like this." Mason's voice was full of conviction.

"You do it well. You were obviously meant to do this." Miranda knew that as well as she knew her own heart. She knew that Mason was a warrior through and through.

Mason gazed at her for a few moments before she spoke. "I do it for the same reason you do your work. It isn't a job; it's a calling. I do it to make my heart feel good."

Miranda's smile bloomed on her face, and Mason's breath caught in her throat as she stared at her. She was so unbelievably beautiful that it was overwhelming. This kind of distraction was the last thing Mason needed right now.

"Let's go to the other conference room. The rest of the team is there, and we can try to answer all your questions."

Miranda stood up after gathering her briefcase and notes together and followed Mason out of the room. Miranda was surprised all over again to find Mason so well dressed. Somehow she thought that cops would dress a little tougher, but there was nothing tough looking about Mason in her stylish pantsuit and silk shirt. With a slight smile playing around her lips, she followed Mason. She knew this was another of Mason's tests to see if she was really who she said she was. Miranda didn't mind; she expected a lot of skepticism from the police. She'd run into it every time she worked with them, her work spoke for itself when she was able to help them solve a case.

"Ms. O'Malley, these are the key members of the task force, and I hope we can answer your questions. These are Detectives Matt Gains, Rick Harper, and Angie Martin. Ben you've met, and this is Agent Johnson. Team, Ms. O'Malley has agreed to help us. She's read the files and has some questions. Hopefully, later today, she's going to go with me to speak with the first two children."

"Before we get started, can I ask you a question, Ms. O'Malley?" Matt inquired his handsome face open and friendly.

"Certainly." She smiled at him. "But please call me Miranda."

Matt wasn't immune to the beautiful woman, and he grinned at her. "Miranda, you're a psychic, right?"

"You could call me that. I'm really a child psychologist, with a few extra skills."

"What can you do?"

Miranda didn't mind answering his questions because she knew they were founded in curiosity. She could tell that Matt was a nice man; nothing but positive energy came from him.

"I'm capable of connecting to people through their emotions. When I make a connection, I can sometimes see flashes of things they're thinking or feeling. I can often see what has happened to them."

"Wow, does it just happen or do you have to work at it?"

"Would you like a demonstration?"

"Sure."

Mason sat quietly watching Miranda interact with the team. She was waiting to see their response to her abilities. Miranda focused her mind and relaxed, breathing slowly as she looked directly at Matt.

"You and your wife are due to have a baby girl within the month. She's a healthy baby and you both want to name her Bryn after your wife's grandmother."

Matt's mouth dropped open in surprise.

Suddenly, Miranda turned to face Mason.

"You didn't give me all the files. Something crucial was withheld from what I read. Something to do with a piece of dark cloth caught somewhere. It's an important piece of the puzzle that might help determine who the kidnapper is."

Mason was surprised at Miranda's statement, but she tried not to show it. She *had* held out the evidence report on the strand of navy blue nylon.

"Matt, would you go grab the notes from my desk?"

"He's going to take another child." Miranda spoke softly, and her eyes slid closed as she focused inward. "He's not getting a big enough thrill from what he's doing, and he's going to kill a child if you don't stop him soon. He's done this before. The children are objects to him, toys he can play with. They don't count. He's playing the game with *you*, Detective Riley. You're the one he's focused on. He wants to show you how smart he is. He thinks he's smarter than everyone. He's laughing because he has you running around looking for him. He's not human inside; he's evil and he won't stop unless you stop him. He's close, very close."

"He left notes with the first two children calling what he's doing a game."

Mason hadn't included the notes left with the children calling what he's doing a game.

Miranda opened her eyes and looked at Mason, her eyes wide and a brilliant green. "That's all it is to him. They are a means to an end. He enjoys hurting them but he also enjoys throwing in your faces the fact that he is out there and you can't stop him. He is stalking these children. He knows them before he takes them and that's why they don't put up a fight. He's looking for another child right now, even though he just took one. He grows bored quickly with one and has to find another plaything. He wants them to fight him. When they don't, he doesn't want them anymore. He's around many children, and he has a job where people trust him. No one around him would ever suspect him."

Miranda hissed in a breath and closed her eyes again. "What he does to those children is abominable! You must stop him! You will stop him!" Her face had gone pasty white, her hands trembling on the table in front of her.

The team wore faces reflecting shock, surprise, and amazement as she spoke, none of them doubting what she had said. Matt's kind and loving heart made him place his large, capable hands on Miranda's to comfort her. He was shocked at how cold her hands were. Mason's eyes hadn't left Miranda's face, and she had seen flashes of pain and despair as she spoke. There was no doubt in Mason's mind that Miranda felt the children's pain. It fascinated her that someone could have such a talent, and it amazed her that she no longer felt it was odd.

A knock on the door interrupted them, and another detective entered, handing Mason a note. She scanned it quickly and looked up. "Miranda, we have a ten-thirty appointment with our first victim. I'm still waiting on a return call from our second victim's parents."

"I need to understand exactly what happened to each child and how they were found. It will help me help them," Miranda responded, her eyes watching Mason's face intently.

"The team can answer your questions. I need to go meet with the Chief before we go any further." Mason strode out of the room.

Miranda pulled her note pad out and turned to the team. She had a lot of work to do.

Chapter 7

"Can you tell me something about this little boy's parents?" Miranda asked as Mason concentrated on driving to the home of the first child. They hadn't said a word on their way to the car as both women prepared mentally and emotionally for the upcoming meeting. Besides, Miranda had a hard time being around Mason since she needed to concentrate on the child; Mason's car was too full of emotions that intruded on her thoughts.

"His father works as a Metro bus driver and his mother is a grade school teacher. They are a loving couple that was almost destroyed when their only child was kidnapped and tortured. Both parents have taken time off from work to help their son heal. The father calls me every day to ask me about the progress on the case." Mason's voice didn't change, but Miranda sensed that she grieved for the parents and the little boy that had been terrified into silence. "Before he was taken, their family was close to perfect."

Miranda understood what Mason was trying to say. Their lives would never be the same again. "He hasn't said a word?"

"He hasn't even cried."

Miranda's eyes filled with tears, her heart aching for the little boy. "What did you tell the parents about why we wanted to see them?"

"I told them you are a child psychologist who works with young children who have been physically or mentally injured. They're hoping that you can help Tanner speak to them."

"Mason, I don't know if I can do that."

Mason turned and looked at Miranda, her eyes gentle with understanding. "But you will try."

Miranda stared at the woman who seemed to understand her so completely. "I'll try."

Mason pulled up in front of a small, well-maintained home in Ballard. The yard was immaculate, and the house was freshly painted with lots of curb appeal. The look was completely deceiving because the young family that lived there was completely devastated. The two women climbed the front porch stairs and, before Mason could knock, a smiling young man opened the door.

"Detective Riley, come on in. Cheryl and Tanner are in the kitchen."

"Thanks, Mr. Boyd. I appreciate you and your family making time for our visit this morning." Mason shook his hand and entered the spotless home, Miranda following in her wake. "This is Ms. O'Malley, the woman I told you about on the telephone."

"Hello, Ms. O'Malley. Please come on back into the kitchen."

Miranda shook the father's hand and casually scanned his thoughts. He was praying that she could help his son. The utter despair in the man's heart made Miranda's own heart hurt. He was at a loss as to what to do to help his son and it was breaking his heart.

"Cheryl, Detective Riley and Ms. O'Malley are here."

"Hello, Detective Riley, Ms. O'Malley, please take a seat. Can I get you some coffee, tea, or anything?" Miranda's heart shuddered. This was a fractured family looking for someone to heal its wounds. Though the kitchen was bright and cheerful, the room bombarded her with anger, sadness, and terror.

"No thanks, Ms. Boyd. Hello, Tanner, are you coloring?" Mason sat down across from the tiny little boy who looked up at her with wounded eyes.

Miranda had been linking with the mother and had found a heart so full of pain and sorrow for her son that Miranda could barely keep her reactions to herself.

Miranda sat down and waited to see what Tanner's reaction would be. He kept his eyes on Mason, watching her with total concentration. Miranda didn't get any indications of fear from him as he watched Mason. She could tell he felt safe with her, but something black and dreadful lay just beneath the surface of his thoughts. "Ms. O'Malley, Detective Riley said you work with children who have been hurt. Can you help us talk to Tanner?" Mrs. Boyd grasped Miranda's hand tightly. "We'll do anything to help him."

Miranda turned, grasped Mrs. Boyd's hand and spoke softly to her. She recognized the utter pain the young mother was dealing with and she hoped she could help her. "I will try to alleviate his fears. He needs to feel safe and be able to trust that no one else will do him any harm. It will take time for him to heal."

"Please help us help him." Mrs. Boyd started to sob, and her husband wrapped his arms around his wife's shoulders trying to console her. His own face looked stricken. No matter what he did he couldn't erase the suffering of his wife and child.

Miranda stood up and went over to kneel next to Tanner, who turned to watch her with his empty eyes. They were completely devoid of emotion. Miranda didn't try to touch him, but she slowed down her breathing and focused her mind on Tanner, closing off everything but him. She gasped as she got glimpses of what the little boy had been subjected to. Although he no longer had any external signs of torture, his internal wounds were still raw. It might be years before he would be able to recuperate and he would carry the horror with him for the rest of his life. No child, no *person* should have to carry such a heavy burden.

"Tanner, he can't hurt you anymore. And I promise you that he won't hurt your mom and dad. Detective Riley will protect all of you. Detective Riley is very good at her job." Miranda's voice was low and soothing, and the little boy looked at her intently as she spoke to him. "He was a very bad man, and it's okay to be mad and angry. He was very sick and it wasn't your fault that he came and took you. You did nothing wrong, honey. You're a very good little boy and I know your parents love you very much. They feel so badly that he came and took you. They looked for you every day you were missing. Your parents did everything they could to find you. Detective Riley looked all over for you."

Mason watched Miranda speaking to the little boy so softly she could barely hear the words, but she knew Tanner was listening. His fingers had dropped his crayon and had moved close to where Miranda's lay on the table next to his.

"Tanner, you're safe now, and I'm so sorry that that bad man took you. I know you're a good little boy. And I can tell that your mom and dad want you to know how very proud they are that you were so brave and came home to them. He can't hurt you any more, sweetie."

Miranda gasped as she saw what the little boy had been told would happen to his parents if he spoke to anyone. "He won't harm your mom and dad. Detective Riley is very good at her job and she is going to catch him and put him in jail for good. He won't ever hurt you or your family again."

Mason smiled as she saw Tanner's fingers slide slowly against Miranda's, his eyes starting to focus on her face. Miranda opened her hand so that Tanner could place his hand in hers. "You are safe, sweetie. And you need to tell your parents how scared you are, so that they understand. They love you very much and want to talk to you. It's okay to be mad and scared, but you need to tell your dad so he can hold you and tell you how much he loves you. Your mom needs to hear you tell her you love her. She was so scared and worried when you were taken."

Tanner turned and looked at his mom and dad who watched their son responding for the first time in several weeks. His eyes were focusing on them, not looking through them.

"We love you, Tanner, very much, and we will keep you safe."

Tanner sighed loudly, almost as if a weight was being lifted from his frail body.

"Tanner, can you do me a favor?" Miranda spoke again, recognizing that the little boy wanted badly to speak to his mom and dad. "Can you whisper to your parents and tell them how much you love them?"

Tanner turned and stared at Miranda for a very long time, and Mason wasn't sure that he was going to respond at all. Slowly, he turned to his parents, and his lips moved as he whispered so quietly that nothing could be heard. But his parents knew what he was trying to say, and both their faces were streaked with tears.

"We love you so very much," his father whispered back, as he watched his only child struggle to overcome unspeakable terror to speak to them. "It's okay to be scared and mad, but we won't let anything happen to you."

Tanner's lips moved again as he tried to talk to his parents. The little boy was still holding Miranda's fingers as tightly as he could grip. "Tanner, that's good. You tell your parents how scared you are. They need to know."

Mason's heart turned over in her chest as the little boy voiced his fear for the first time. His father bent over and gathered his tiny son in his arms while tears rolled freely down his face. "I know you're scared, and it's okay, son. We'll protect you. You're safe now."

Tanner's arms locked around his father's neck as he held on with every bit of strength he had in his body. His mother wrapped her arms around her husband and son and they rocked together for several minutes, trying to heal their wounded family. Miranda's eyes glistened with tears, as she remained kneeling next to Mason. Mason had to turn away from the family to maintain her composure. Miranda reached up and tucked her fingers into Mason's and squeezed gently in comfort. Mason felt her emotions settle as she held on to Miranda's hand. She was amazed at how quickly Miranda had managed to help the young boy and his family during one short visit. It was nothing short of miraculous.

"Ms. O'Malley, we can't thank you enough." Mr. Boyd spoke as he placed his son in his wife's arms.

"I didn't do a thing. Your son is a very brave little boy and he wanted to tell you he loves you." Miranda released Mason's hand as she stood up.

"I still want to thank you. Do you think you might have some time for Tanner, his mother, and me to meet with you? I think you could help us some more."

"I'll make the time. I counsel only children, but I can help you help him. Here's my card. Please call and make an appointment that's convenient for the three of you." Miranda smiled at the young father. "Mr. Boyd, you and your wife need to talk to Tanner as much as possible about how angry you are. He needs to know it's okay to be mad. He still thinks he has to protect you and you need to help him understand he's safe."

"We will."

"Mr. and Mrs. Boyd, we'll be leaving now. Thank you for making the time to see us." Mason spoke calmly although she felt like screaming. She was so angry that Tanner and his family had to cope with all of this.

"Detective Riley, thank you for bringing Ms. O'Malley; we'll do anything we can to help you solve this case."

"You and your wife take care of Tanner. He's such a courageous little boy." Mason smiled at the small child. "Tanner, you're safe now, and so are your parents. I promise you, I'm going to catch the man who hurt you and I'll lock him away forever."

Miranda and Mason exited the house after Tanner's father hugged them both goodbye. He was overwhelmed with gratefulness. Miranda got into Mason's car and tried to keep her emotions in check, but to no avail. Scorching tears ran down her face unchecked as sobs, no longer silent, convulsed her body. Mason turned to Miranda and gathered her up in her arms as Miranda wept uncontrollably. Mason's face was covered with her own tears as she grieved for the little boy and his parents.

"How do you do it?"

"Do what?" Mason whispered as she held Miranda, her fingers stroking her neck in an attempt to soothe the distraught woman.

"See families like that destroyed by some sick pervert. What he did to Tanner is abominable. That little boy is going to be frightened for a very long time."

"I _will_ catch him, Miranda."

"I know that. It's just so sad to see such a wonderful family in so much turmoil."

"Yes, it is. I'll catch the man that did this and I'll put him in jail so he'll never touch another child."

Miranda had stopped crying and was content to be held in Mason's arms where she felt safe and protected. "You're good at your job because it's important to you to protect others."

"I like being a good cop."

Miranda smiled and pulled slowly away from Mason, admiring the pretty woman who took on such heavy responsibility. "We'd better get back to your office. I need to write down what I got from Tanner."

Mason turned and started her car. "Did you get something from him?"

"I think so, but I need to collect my thoughts and get it down on paper before I share it with you. Everything is in bits and pieces. I do know that that this man knew Tanner before he took him. I saw a tall, dark man, his face fuzzy, but he was wearing a uniform, a dark uniform of some sort. Tanner wasn't scared of him until after he took him. What he did to Tanner turns my stomach. He's twisted. His mind isn't normal. He gets off on hurting children."

Mason glanced at Miranda and saw that her face was pale and drawn with worry. "Miranda, Tanner is safe."

"But this creep has another child."

"We'll find her, Miranda. I won't quit until I find April."

Miranda remained silent as she continued to go over all the images she had received from Tanner. She was quiet for the rest of the trip back to the police precinct. Mason and Miranda entered the conference room where the rest of the task team was assembled going over report after report.

"Hey, Mason, Ms. O'Malley, how did the meeting go?"

"I'd like to spend some time writing down my impressions before reviewing with the team, if you don't mind," Miranda answered, her mind already working on organizing what she'd been able to capture from Tanner's feelings. Because Miranda captured disjointed images, not everything would be relevant to exactly what they were looking for. Hopefully, she could sort through it all and try and make some sense of it.

"No problem," Matt responded. "I'm sending out for lunch. What would the two of you like?"

After ordering a sandwich, Miranda sat down at the table, pulled her notebook out of her briefcase and began writing. Mason went to her desk and responded to the messages that had come in while she was gone. An hour later, Mason headed back to the conference room for lunch. She was surprised to see Miranda and Matt standing at the whiteboard, discussing the case.

"Matt, he's had contact with these children before he took them. He knows them, which is why he can get them to go with him without incident. He wears some kind of dark uniform and is tall, with short, dark hair. I can't pull his face out of the images but I get the impression that he is charming and friendly. He hides his dark side very well."

"Okay, we need to make the connection between Tanner's abduction and the other two. Somewhere, the cases overlap."

"It's there somewhere, I just can't pull it out of my head," Miranda sighed as she continued to look at the board trying to pick up on something. "I just can't quite get it."

"Lunch is here. Why don't you take a break?" Mason announced, as another detective unloaded two large bags of food onto the table. "Come on guys, lunch."

Miranda and Matt turned and both smiled at Mason as they walked toward the table. The beautiful woman standing across the table from her struck Mason silent. Her smile was amazing, as were her laughing eyes. She and Matt were sharing something that made them both laugh, and Mason knew that Matt liked Miranda; it showed in his body language.

The team sat down and quickly began devouring deli sandwiches as they chatted. Mason remained quiet, observing the team as they stepped away from their onerous jobs for a brief time. Matt and Miranda were visiting back and forth about Matt's impending fatherhood and his excitement about the upcoming event.

"Jena and I have the room all ready and Mason has filled it with toys. Every time she comes over she brings a new toy for her niece."

"Are you and Mason related?"

"Not by marriage, but she's our kid's aunt and godmother. She was my best man at our wedding and Jena would adopt her if she could."

Mason rolled her eyes at Matt's comment. Mason surprised them both with her smiling comment. "His wife needs all your sympathy after marrying Matt. It took him a year to propose to Jena and now he's already planning what college his little girl is going to attend. Jena needs someone with a level head around her."

Miranda couldn't stop the laughter that rolled out of her. Mason loved Matt and his wife, but she was embarrassed that Matt had revealed that to Miranda. Mason was startled by Miranda's laughter. It was full and robust, and the sexiest thing Mason had heard in ages. It made her body heat up uncontrollably. She was surprised that no one else had the same reaction as she did. The woman was gorgeous, sexy, and fascinating. How could they not react to her?

Mason's cell phone rang, preventing any further comment. "Detective Riley Yes, we can be there within an hour. Yes, I understand."

Mason turned to Miranda, her eyes once again serious, and focused on her job. "That was the father of Tammy Webster, the little four-year old girl that was found several days ago. We can go see Tammy at the hospital if we get there by one. His wife is already there and he's going to meet us. He'll give us thirty minutes with his daughter."

"Is he okay with my seeing his child?"

"He and his wife are extremely worried about their little girl, but he did agree to have you see her for a short time. He's very angry, especially at the police department for not catching the garbage before his little girl was taken. Frankly, I'm surprised he's letting us near her."

Miranda stared at Mason for a brief moment before dropping her eyes. "I need to reread the files on Tammy before I see her."

Mason pulled out Tammy Webster's file and handed it to Miranda. She took it from her with a big sigh, settling her breathing to calm herself. Once again, she opened a file and focused on the information in front of her. She knew the memories of the little girl would be strong, full of pain and suffering. She needed to be prepared.

Chapter 8

Miranda and Mason didn't say anything on the quick drive to Children's Orthopedic Hospital. Neither one noticed the sparkling water of Lake Washington or the University campus as they passed it. And neither one was ready to discuss their impending interview with the four-year-old girl. Miranda was focused and prepared. They entered the hospital and Mason led the way to the second floor room. She didn't have to tell Miranda that she had been to the room several times before today. The little girl lay quietly on the hospital bed, a woman seated next to her reading a story. A young man stood behind the woman, his hand resting on her shoulder. They both looked up at Mason and Miranda as they entered the flower-and balloon-filled hospital room. The man's face flashed anger and his eyes watched their entry closely. Miranda didn't need to be told they weren't wanted, The man's anger filled the room.

"Mr. and Mrs. Webster, this is Miranda O'Malley. Miranda, this is Mr. and Mrs. Webster and their daughter, Tammy. Mason moved close to the bed and smiled at the petite girl who watched her approach. "Hi, Tammy."

Miranda smiled hello to the parents and turned to smile at the little girl. Her breath caught in her throat as she gazed down at the little girl whose body still showed physical signs of her abuse. Her wrists were black and blue with bruising from her restraints, and haunted eyes stared out of her equally bruised and battered face. She was such a tiny thing sitting in the clinical hospital bed, but it was her eyes that broke Miranda's heart. She was looking at the saddest and most poignant child she'd ever witnessed.

"Tammy, is it okay if I sit down next to you?"

Tammy stared at the pretty woman who spoke so softly and sat in the empty chair by her bed. She didn't acknowledge that she had heard a word, but her eyes were fixed on Miranda's face.

"Tammy, I'm so glad to see you safe and back with your parents. They were so worried about you and they didn't stop looking for you while you were lost. They love you and they were so scared while everyone looked for you."

Miranda watched the delicate little girl for any signs of fear or discomfort, but she showed absolutely nothing. She took several deep breaths to calm herself and then slowed down her breathing and heart rate and opened herself up to Tammy's feelings. After reading the doctor's report of the little girl's abuse, Miranda had thought she was ready, but nothing could have prepared her for the horrors still flickering in Tammy's subconscious. She was terrified, her mind filled with the blackness of evil. It was hard to stay connected as Miranda shared the suffering that the little girl had been subjected to. Pain coursed through her body, and it took all her effort not to cry out as she trembled, her control barely intact.

"Tammy, I know you're very angry at that evil man for what he did. I am too. When I get angry I take a pillow and I slap it really hard. Can I show you?"

Miranda picked up the spare pillow and held it toward Mason. "Detective Riley, will you hold this pillow for me?"

Mason held the pillow up for Miranda as she observed Tammy watching Miranda very closely. She was hoping Miranda could get through to the little girl. "Tammy, when I'm really, really mad, I slap my pillow as hard as I can. Like this."

Miranda reached up and slapped the pillow. She knew how important it was for a very young child to release her anger. If allowed to fester, it would hamper her recovery. Anger was a healthy emotion in an abused child and needed an outlet. "Sometimes I hit it over and over again."

She hit the pillow a few more times while Tammy's solemn eyes watched her every move. "Do you think you could hit this pillow for me to show me how mad you are?"

Tammy watched Miranda but she didn't move. "You know what, Tammy? Your dad is very mad at the bad man who hurt you. I bet he'd like to hit the pillow."

Miranda turned to Tammy's father and smiled. "Mr. Webster, Tammy knows you're very angry that she was hurt. Can you punch this pillow and show Tammy how angry you are? She needs to see that it's okay to be angry."

His anger emanated from him in waves, and Mason wasn't sure that Tammy's father was going to do as Miranda had asked. He couldn't see beyond his daughter's hideous injuries. He stared daggers into Miranda's eyes. Then something made his face soften and he sighed. Tammy's father punched the pillow forcefully and looked at his daughter. "I'm very sad and angry that you were taken from your mom and me."

"Okay, Tammy, it's your turn. You show us how angry you are by punching this pillow."

Tammy looked up at her dad and then her little hand slowly formed a fist, and she reached up and punched at the pillow that Mason held. "Good job, Tammy. Now, let's see you punch it even harder."

Mason felt the rush of emotion as Tammy's little fist punched the pillow again. She turned to watch Miranda's face as she gazed at the little girl who was trying so hard to communicate her feelings.

"Good job, Tammy. You hit the pillow again and again."

Tammy lifted both of her tiny arms, her fingers clenched into fists, and over and over she pummeled the pillow that Mason held. Her breathing became labored, her chest rising and falling as she flailed at the pillow. She began to grunt as she struck it over and over, her anger unleashed at last. A dam had burst and her fury exploded. Both parents were crying as were Miranda and Mason while they watched the little girl communicate for the first time since she had been found lying naked in her own blood.

Tammy's blows began to diminish in frequency and intensity as she ran out of steam and began to cry deep gulping sobs. Her mother rushed to the bed and wrapped her arms around Tammy, rocking her back and forth as she tried to soothe her daughter. Tammy's father stood by his wife as he watched his little girl cry against her mother's shoulder. Miranda placed her hand on Mr. Webster's arm. "It's very healthy that she's crying."

Tammy's father looked sorrowfully down at Miranda. "I know. She hasn't cried since we found her."

"For the next couple of weeks, I would like you to hold a pillow up for Tammy to punch every night. You and your wife should hit it too, to show her how angry you still are. She needs to be able to release her emotions and she's too young to understand or talk about what's wrong. She'll start talking when she's ready. She needs to feel safe again. She doesn't understand what has happened to her. She thinks she did something wrong. If you can tell her she's a good girl as often as possible, it will go far to helping her heal."

Mr. Webster looked down at his little girl who, for the first time since she'd been abducted, was looking at him instead of staring blankly at him, and he smiled with tears in his eyes. "I can't thank you enough for what you did."

"I just pointed the way. Your daughter is a courageous child. I would strongly suggest that you and your wife get some help, along with your daughter. I can recommend a counselor, if you're interested."

"Can *you* see us? Tammy responded to you, and we have the money."

"Mr. Webster, I would certainly be available to help you with Tammy, but I don't counsel adults. I know some excellent counselors that I could recommend."

"We'd appreciate that very much. Please leave your information. We do want to bring Tammy to you."

"Here's my business card. Call me any time." Miranda smiled at the gentle man who wanted more than anything to help his daughter heal. She understood his anger. "Thank you for letting us visit with you and your daughter. She's a valiant little girl."

"We can't thank you enough." He hugged Miranda tightly and then hugged Mason, his face covered with tears.

Miranda and Mason quietly left the room and were seated in the car within minutes. Miranda was so overwhelmed she couldn't speak. It was Mason who exploded as she pounded her fists on the steering wheel. "Goddamn it! I have got to catch this bastard! He can't get away with this! Shit! Shit! Shit!"

Miranda remained quiet as she watched Mason vent her feelings. She wasn't surprised at Mason's anger. She had been holding it in all day. Mason turned to look at Miranda and she grimaced as she spoke. "Sorry. I'm just so frustrated."

"Honey, you don't have to apologize. I feel like crying my eyes out." Miranda's eyes overflowed with tears and Mason's heart reacted. She reached out and gathered Miranda into her arms as she started to cry. These weren't like the earlier sobs; this was deep, painful weeping that came from heartbreak and sorrow. Mason held the woman until she stopped her heart-wrenching crying, content just to hold her tightly, offering comfort.

"I seem to be crying on your shoulder a lot today."

"That's okay," Mason whispered as she stared at a woman who continued to astound her.

"We need to get back to the office so I can describe what I saw in Tammy's memories."

"Did you get more information?"

"He was the same tall, dark, short-haired man. He wasn't wearing a uniform; it looked like an athletic suit, and I could see a set of bleachers in the background.

I think it was a sports field or something similar. He knew her before he took her, because I don't see any fear until after she was taken. He wore a mask when he hurt her, and I can't see his face, but Mason, what he did to that little girl is ghastly. She was in so much pain. He hurt her so badly, and he threatened to kill her parents if she told anyone his name. He terrified her with pain and abuse. I can't imagine how frightened she was when he hurt her. What kind of animal is capable of this?" Miranda held tightly to Mason's hand as she spoke.

"Let's get back to the office and get you with a sketch artist. Maybe we can get enough of a likeness that someone will recognize him." Mason let Miranda's hands go and turned to start the car. Both women remained silently lost in their own thoughts as they rode back to the precinct. They were both emotionally drained after seeing the two children and their devastated parents.

"How did the interview go?" Ben asked, as he and Ann sat in the conference room. They had been trying to identify any connections between the children that they could follow up on. Matt was at his desk making telephone calls; then joined them in the conference room.

"I need to get a sketch artist to work with Miranda. Miranda, do you want to explain to the team what you were able to pick up?"

"Certainly, but do you think I could use the restroom first, if you don't mind?" Miranda looked ashen.

"Here, I'll show you where the bathroom is," Ann smiled and directed Miranda down the hall.

"Mason, Miranda looks awfully pale."

"She's been through a lot today," Mason shared with Matt. "Both children responded to her. It was incredible."

"She's an unbelievable lady."

"Yes, she is."

Mason went to her desk for a few minutes until she saw Miranda returning to the conference room. Ann came up to her and spoke under her breath. "Mason, Miranda was violently ill in the bathroom."

"Did you help her?"

"As much as I could, but Miranda still looks way too pale."

"I'll speak to her." Mason re-entered the room and approached Miranda who sat at the table writing furiously on her tablet. Her face was pale and beaded with sweat.

Mason sat down next to her and spoke just loudly enough to get her attention. "Miranda, are you okay?"

Miranda looked up at Mason, her eyes wounded as she gazed at her. "I'll be fine. I think I should share what I know with the team now, before I forget anything."

"Miranda..."

"Mason, I'll be fine, really." Miranda placed her hand on Mason's and squeezed gently. Mason was startled by the icy coldness of her hands. She fought the urge to slip her arms around Miranda and hug her. For some reason she wanted to protect her from any more pain. "Thanks."

Mason smiled at her and slowly stood up. "Okay, team, Miranda would like to explain to you what she knows."

They all grew silent and waited expectantly for Miranda to speak. They knew that Miranda was working hard to help them.

"I was able to glimpse the same tall, dark-haired man that Tanner saw. He was wearing a sports sweat suit at some time while he was with Tammy. I could also see a set of bleachers in the background when he was talking to her. He knew Tammy before he took her. She wasn't afraid of him until he started hurting her and then he terrorized her. He did such painful and sickening things to her. He hurt her so badly." Miranda's eyes squeezed shut as she spoke, her hands clenched together tightly on the table in front of her. "He hurts these children because he can. Over and over he hurt her, and he told her he would kill her and her parents if she said anything."

The room was silent as Miranda continued to speak. The colleagues at the table shared feelings of shock and disbelief that were reflected on their faces. "He had her chained to a cot somewhere in a small, dark room. He can't stand fully upright when he's in it. She was left there for long periods of time, and then he would come back and give her a little food and water before he would start hurting her again. She didn't cry after a couple of days because he didn't like it when she cried. She gave up waiting for her parents to find her. He broke her spirit, and she was no longer any fun to play with, so he left her somewhere she could be found. He wants people to know what he's doing. It's part of his game. He wanted a new toy to play with so he kidnapped this latest little girl. He doesn't want them if they don't continue to fight him. He hurts them because he enjoys it, and he will kill a child sooner or later. That thought in his head already. It's just a matter of time before he acts on it."

Miranda took a big, deep breath and began to speak again, the emotion in her voice making it fade in and out. "He's around children a lot. He knows them well, and they trust him. He has a job working with children or he has a lot of contact with them. He might be a coach, a teacher, someone who has a job where people trust him. He might wear a navy blue uniform. I just can't quite place it, but it's familiar. If only I could figure it out!"

Miranda bowed her head and stopped talking. The people assembled in the room just stared at her, recognizing the enormous effort Miranda was putting into trying to help them identify the man. Her hands were clenched tightly together; her face was taut with pain and sorrow.

Matt was the first to speak, his voice gentle as he reached out and covered Miranda's hands, rubbing her cold hands between his own. "Miranda, we'll find him. Let's get the sketch artist to work on a composite while I continue to make my telephone calls. You've given us a lot to work on. Something's going to pop, I know it."

"Thanks, Matt. Do you think I could get a cup of hot tea?" Miranda needed something to ease her nausea.

"Sure, we'll stop and get you one on our way to the identification unit."

Mason watched as Matt and Miranda walked out of the room together. She was worried about Miranda. This case was taking a toll on her.

"Mason, she's amazing. I really think she's got something. We need to discover what those three families had in common. There's something there, I know it!"

"Keep working on it, Ben. I'll get the night shift to go over our reports too. Sometimes a new set of eyes sees something we've missed. I need to go update the Chief and write my report for today. You guys need to get out of here and get a good night's sleep. You've been here almost twelve hours."

"We'll go when you go." Ben smiled at the exhausted detective. His respect for Mason grew daily.

"I'll be with the Chief."

Chapter 9

"Come in!" The bellow was loud and sounded decidedly unfriendly, but Mason knew better. The Chief always sounded upset but he rarely was.

"Chief, do you have a moment so I can update you on the case?"

"Are you any closer to catching this creep?"

"We're still looking for connections between the two children's families."

"Find one, goddamn it!"

Mason wasn't offended by his tone or his anger. "Chief, can I use some of the night shift to go over our files and reports? We need a new set of eyes on this case. We're missing something."

"Go ahead, on one condition."

"And that is?" Mason was used to the Chief's conditions; he always had at least one.

"That you and your team get out of here and get a good night's sleep. Let the night shift guys work the cases. Your team is running on fumes. You all need a good night's rest."

"I'll get them out of here."

"I didn't just say your team. I'm expecting *you* to go home and get a good night's sleep."

"But, Chief…"

"That's my condition, take it or leave it." The Chief glared at Mason and she knew he wouldn't budge.

"I'll take it; thanks, Chief."

"Get out and go home!"

Mason grinned as she left the Chief of Detective's office. The Chief was a hard working, good man, who cared a lot about his detectives. She thought again about how much she liked and respected him.

Mason returned to the conference room and sat down with Ann and Ben and a stack of interview notes. Matt returned a few minutes later and joined them. He sat down next to Mason, and she knew something was on his mind. He didn't have the usual smile on his face. He was always smiling.

"Matt, what's up, buddy?"

Matt turned to his partner and his best friend and he sighed. "I'm worried about Miranda, Mason. Did you know when she connects with someone who has memories of being hurt that she can feel their physical pain? She felt every single thing that Tammy experienced."

"I didn't know that." Mason felt like she'd been punched in the stomach. She'd had no idea.

"She felt everything, Mason. I can't believe she didn't tell you." Matt's voice broke as his compassion for Miranda touched him. He hated that she was hurting.

Mason knew what she would have done had she had this information before. She would have stopped the meeting. She wouldn't have let Miranda be hurt. Mason was also sure that Miranda had known that, and she had purposely kept that knowledge from Mason. Mason was going to have a serious conversation with her. "I'll talk to her, Matt."

"Good. I really like Miranda. She's a very generous person."

"Yes, she is."

Matt grabbed the interview notes and smiled down at his partner. "Where are we?"

"We're still going back over the case files from the first kidnapping. We're looking for any references to sports, teams, coaching…anything like that."

Chapter 10

"Miranda, do you mind my asking you about your psychic abilities?"

The sketch artist or identification technician, as she preferred to be called, was a young, energetic woman who peppered Miranda with questions as she manipulated the computer. The slender woman, whose designer jeans and tee shirt looked slightly out of place, was obviously delighted with her job and with meeting Miranda. Contrary to what Miranda expected, most of the sketching was done with special software to develop a composite drawing of the suspect. Miranda was fascinated with the process and Lois, the technician, was enthralled by the fact that Miranda was a bona fide psychic.

"Not at all." Miranda smiled at the young woman with the purple steak in her hair. Lois almost bounced in her chair next to a very sedate Miranda.

"So...what do you do?"

Miranda bubbled with laughter as she caught a glimpse of what Lois thought a psychic might do. "If I link with someone, I can read their feelings, emotions, and sometimes their memories."

"Wow, that's cool. Do you, like, see everything like a movie?"

"Not as clearly as that. I see flashes of images out of context. Sometimes I can make sense of it, sometimes I can't. It depends on how strong a person's emotions or feelings are. If they've been hurt or scared, the images tend to be clearer and stronger and easier for me to connect with."

"So do you, like, pick up on stuff all the time?"

"No. I have to open myself up to reading someone and I don't do it randomly." Miranda didn't tell her how difficult it had been as a child not to pick up on everything swirling around her. "I won't read adults unless they ask me to or if

I'm helping a child. I work with children who have experienced some form of trauma and are finding it difficult to heal. I help them understand their fears and anger and deal with them."

"Why children?"

"Because most of the time they don't have the skills we have to cope with what has happened to them. They're much more open and easier for me to read. They're also in need of someone who can help them, sometimes without their knowing it."

"That's so cool." The young woman looked at Miranda with awe. "Could you, could you do me a favor?"

Miranda grinned at her. "You want me to give you a demonstration."

"Please?"

Miranda closed her eyes and tried to concentrate. She was extremely tired after the long emotional day. The children's interviews had drained her. Slowly she breathed in and out, settling herself, and opened her mind, focusing on Lois, who sat next to her, completely mesmerized and, for the moment, still.

"You're thinking of moving in with your boyfriend, but you're worried that he isn't as serious about the relationship as you are. You just received a promotion and enjoy your job, but you're thinking about going back to school for more training in computer forensics. You and your best friend are going out tonight for drinks and dancing and you think I'm pretty cool for a psychic." Miranda opened her eyes and grinned at Lois. The young woman was so engaging. Lois sat in her chair, her mouth hanging open in complete disbelief.

"Wow, I mean…wow! That is so amazing. You must be rich! You could do anything with that."

Miranda couldn't help but laugh at the young woman's comments. "I'm not rich. I have a degree in psychology, and I don't use my abilities to make money. It goes against everything I believe in."

"Cool; are you the only one or do you come from a long line of psychics?"

"My grandmother's mother was gifted, as are my grandmother and my mother."

"So if you had a kid, she'd like be a psychic too?"

"Probably."

"I bet you got teased a lot when you were growing up."

"Kids sometimes teased me, but my mother intervened, and most times she was successful in stopping it. In my grandmother's day, she could have been jailed or put to death if people believed she was a witch."

"You're kidding me."

"No. Some people aren't open to psychic abilities and believe that they're a sign of witch craft."

"I can't believe anyone who met you would think you're a witch."

"Thank you," Miranda smiled. "How's our composite coming?"

"Good, except that we don't have much detail in the face. I've prepared a bunch of composites using different eyes, noses, and mouths to see if one of them might trigger someone's memory. I'll print up a bunch and bring them down to the conference room when I take you back there."

"Good." Miranda was quickly running out of energy.

"So, do you work with the police a lot?"

"Some, not a whole lot. My mother and grandmother have both worked on many cases."

"Any I know?"

"I'm sure you would, but one thing we don't do is advertise our work."

"Do they do it for a living?"

"No. My mother is an interior designer in New Orleans, and my grandmother owns an antique store there."

"Is that where you grew up?"

"It is."

"What does your father do?"

"He was a lawyer until he passed away several years ago."

"I'm sorry."

"It's not a problem."

"Well, we're done. Let me get those copies and we're out of here."

"Lois, don't worry about moving in with your boyfriend. Everything is going to be fine."

Lois beamed a happy smile at her and leaped out of her chair. "That's so cool, thanks." She wrapped her arms around Miranda and hugged her energetically. Miranda felt a little less tired after being hugged by the charming young woman. "Come on, I promised Matt I'd walk you back to the conference room. Boy, is he one good looking guy."

Miranda just grinned and walked quickly to keep up with the dynamic woman. She did everything at top speed. They made the trip back to the conference room where everyone was quietly reviewing the files. They all looked as tired as Miranda felt.

"Hey, guys, here are the composites for you to distribute. I'll send the electronic files to you when I get back to my desk. Because Miranda was unclear about the face, we tried several different looks."

"Thanks, Lois. We appreciate your staying late and jumping on this."

"No problem, Mason. It was cool working with Miranda. She's unbelievable!" Lois flashed her quick grin and turned to leave. "I'm out of here."

Miranda saw the grin on Mason's face and she smiled back at her. "Does she do anything slowly?"

"Not that I've ever noticed. What about you, Matt?"

"Not since she started working here two years ago."

"She's exhausting, but very sweet," Miranda responded with a chuckle.

"That might have to do with the fact that you've been working since six this morning and it's almost seven o'clock at night."

"You're kidding!" Miranda was shocked at how late it was.

"No, and today must have been very difficult for you," Mason responded, watching Miranda carefully.

"Not any more difficult than it was on the rest of you."

Mason lowered her voice as she responded. "Miranda, why didn't you tell me you would feel physically what Tammy had gone through?"

Miranda flushed with embarrassment as she responded. "It's not as bad as it sounds. It depends on exactly what she had endured and how much time had passed since it happened."

"You felt her pain. I saw it on your face."

"Mason, it's what I do. It is the only way I could help her." Miranda's eyes filled with tears as she tried to explain herself.

"Do you think it's any easier to watch you relive that child's pain? You need to be honest with me."

"I am. That's how my abilities work. I can't control that piece of it."

"I'm sorry."

"I'm not. If I can help any of those children, it's worth it."

"You helped both of them and us. We'll get him," Mason promised, her eyes conveying her emotions and her commitment. "I've been ordered to get this team out of the building for the night. Since you're now officially one of the team, I suggest that as soon as I hand out all the assignments to the night crew, I take you home."

"Sounds good to me," Miranda smiled at the obviously exhausted and emotionally charged detective.

Mason stood up, stretched, and exited the room. She was back in less than ten minutes with several men following in her wake. "Guys, the files are here. Matt and the team have put a lot of the information into the database, but we may have missed something. Key words are *sports, athletics, teams, coaching*, and *parks*—anything to do with those words that might connect the families in some way."

"Got it, Mason. Hey, if we do a good job can you talk to the Chief about moving me to days for a while? My girlfriend is ready to dump me."

"Hah, your girlfriend is ready to dump you because of your looks, not because you're working nights," Matt snorted. "Look in the mirror."

"Hey, she thinks I'm a god!" Detective Ken Murphy fired back.

"She thinks you're a toad!"

"Guys, guys, try to keep it down to a dull roar," Mason asked, grinning at the two of them.

"We can't all be pretty like Matt." Ken fluttered his eyelashes at him.

"Stuff it, Ken." Matt flushed with embarrassment.

"Ken, you're in charge. Call me on my cell if you find anything."

"I will, Mason. Get some sleep before you keel over."

"Come on, Miranda, I'll take you home."

"I'll walk out with you," Matt commented as he grabbed his cell phone and his jacket while Miranda and Mason collected their things. "So, Miranda, are you going to keep working with us?"

"If you need me, I will."

"Good. I think you've been a great help today. Mason told me you really helped both kids a lot. She said you were amazing."

Mason flushed as Matt spoke to Miranda. She wasn't sure what Miranda would think of her opinions. Besides, she was having a difficult time with the fact that she was attracted to her. She'd never experienced anything close to this, especially at work, and it threw her off her game. Miranda glanced at Mason and saw the flush of embarrassment and the scowl she threw Matt's way. Miranda wasn't quite sure what Mason was thinking, but something was bothering her.

Matt hugged both of them goodbye and climbed into his car. He couldn't wait to get home to his wife. Mason and Miranda got into Mason's car and within minutes, Mason was heading toward Miranda's home.

"If I have your address right, you live in those condominiums in Belltown that look out over the water."

"You've got it right."

"How long have you lived there?"

"Almost four years."

"Do you like living downtown?"

"I do. Belltown isn't like living in the city. It's unique and rather like a small neighborhood. Everyone knows everyone and looks out for each other. I lived in an apartment in the same area before I bought my condo. Where do you live?"

"I have an apartment in Ballard. It's close to work and it's quiet."

"How long have you lived there?"

"About eight years. Matt and Jena keep trying to get me to buy a house but I haven't really found one I like that well. Besides, if I had a house I would have to take care of the yard and everything. I just don't have the time to do it all."

"What do you do when you aren't working?"

"I hike and bike ride and I'd like to travel if I had the time. What about you?"

"I like to listen to music, read, and go on long walks."

"Here's your place." Mason pulled up in front of the modern building and turned to face Miranda. "Thank you very much for your time today."

"No problem. Do you think you'll need me again?"

"I think we will, if you're willing, but I can't give you a timeframe yet. Miranda, I know it was very difficult for you today, especially with Tammy. I don't want you to take on something that will cause you any more pain."

"What I felt was nothing compared to what Tammy felt. I'll let you know if it gets to be too much for me. You have my card so you know how to reach me." Miranda didn't want to end her time with Mason. For some reason she needed to be around her a little bit longer. Something had brought the two together, and Miranda wouldn't question fate. "Mason, I'm going to fix a quick dinner for myself. Would you like to join me?"

Mason's look of surprise and flush of pleasure encouraged Miranda. "It's not gourmet cooking, but I think I can provide a fairly decent meal."

Mason smiled back at the beautiful woman who had intrigued her all day long. "I'd like that."

"Good; come on up and let's see what I can whip up," Miranda chuckled, climbing out of the car. Mason followed Miranda into the building and the elevator. "I can't wait to get out of these shoes."

Mason looked down and all but groaned. Miranda had been wearing heels all day long. "Those shoes look great but they must be killing you after wearing them for so many hours."

Miranda flashed a quick grin at Mason. "They are painful."

She walked out of the elevator and moved ahead of Mason to the door of her condominium. From the front lobby and the hallway, Mason could tell that Miranda's home was going to be elegant. The building was impressive. Unlocking the door, Miranda swung inside and held the door open. "Come on in and make yourself at home."

Chapter 11

"Mason, would you like a glass of wine while I warm up the lasagna?" Miranda asked as she placed her briefcase on the floor by the door and kicked off her shoes. Mason followed her into the living room.

"I don't know if I should. I'm so tired I'll probably fall asleep before dinner." Mason was intrigued by the large, open living room. One full wall was all glass facing Puget Sound, and the view was stunning as the sun slowly disappeared below the horizon. Mason stood at the window enjoying the captivating sight. She felt her body start to release some of the stress of the day.

"Sometimes, I just sit here in the evening enjoying the sunset." Miranda's voice was mellow, just like her approach, as she came to stand next to Mason. "When I have a particularly tough day, sitting here somehow helps me to forget."

"It's healing," Mason responded, strongly drawn to the beautiful woman standing within inches of her.

"Yes it is, and we all need a place like that."

"You must be exhausted after your day."

"I'm saddened more than anything. This should never happen to children."

"I've got to find this latest girl." Mason's voice cracked with emotion and tears slid down her face.

"Mason." Miranda wrapped her arms around her slender shoulders, holding her tightly, trying to provide a measure of comfort.

Mason's arms snaked around Miranda as she tucked her face against Miranda's neck. She'd rarely had anyone offer emotional support and she needed it. She was almost to the breaking point with this ghastly case and the missing child. She wept on Miranda's shoulder for several minutes until she felt drained, and then she just clung to Miranda, unwilling to let go. Miranda felt a strong attraction to Mason as she moved her hands slowly up and down Mason's back trying to soothe her. Mason's fingers played with the wavy hair at the base of Miranda's neck. She was acutely aware of Miranda's body pressed tightly to her, wreaking havoc with her emotions. Unable to resist, Mason barely touched her lips to Miranda's neck. Miranda moaned and turned until she met Mason's lips with her own. Mouths meshed, tongues tasted, and need welled up as the two women succumbed to the magnetism that each had felt during the long day.

Mason's mouth covered Miranda's over and over with full kisses that stripped away the last semblance of Miranda's control. Hands slid over breasts and cupped hips, fingers stroking and tracing each other's bodies through their clothes. Miranda struggled to pull Mason's shirt out of her pants, fighting with her shoulder harness, while Mason's shaking hands clumsily unbuttoned Miranda's jacket. Their labored breathing filled the room as they struggled to remove their clothing, intent on one thing and one thing alone.

"Your bedroom, where's your bedroom?" Mason gasped as Miranda's hands found Mason's breasts under her shirt. Mason dropped Miranda's jacket and silk shell to the floor; she pulled her shoulder harness off so that Miranda could slide her shirt off of her shoulders. Mason's lips tasted the skin above Miranda's pale blue bra. Miranda's professional business suit had hidden a voluptuous body that was rapidly being revealed as Mason dropped Miranda's skirt to the floor. Mason moaned loudly as she took a moment to gaze at Miranda's ice blue bra and matching panties. She wore nylons, but not traditional pantyhose. Navy blue garter straps held up her thigh-high nylons, and Mason had never seen anything so damned sexy.

"It's the last room on the right," Miranda whispered as she watched Mason stare at her. "Are you okay with this?"

"Miranda, I want my hands and mouth on your gorgeous body, and if we don't find your bedroom soon it's going to be right here on the living room floor," Mason promised with a smile, as she ran her hands over Miranda's hips and pulled her tightly against her body. "Do you want this?"

"I want you," Miranda laughed as she pulled away from Mason and dragged her down the hall into the darkened bedroom.

Both women swiftly tore off the rest of their clothing as they tumbled onto the bed, Miranda's body pinning Mason to the mattress. Her thigh pressed against Mason's already drenched center while her hot mouth surrounded Mason's nipple. Miranda's tongue and teeth teased Mason, and she made Mason's breasts ache, as she tasted them over and over. Mason's hips rolled against Miranda's, grinding her wetness into Miranda's firm thigh. Miranda's hands moved over the strong, slender body that arched and moved against hers. Mason was overwhelmed as Miranda's lovemaking made her shudder and hunger raged through her body like nothing she'd ever experienced before. Miranda couldn't slow down as the scent of Mason filled the air and made Miranda's mouth water. Her hand slid over the satin skin of Mason's stomach into the ash blond curls that protected Mason's throbbing lips.

"Miranda, please," Mason pleaded as Miranda cupped her, smiling as her fingertips slid into the drenched cavity. Mason gasped as Miranda entered her completely and filled her tightly.

Mason's hips arched as she pushed against Miranda's tightly enclosed fingers. "You're so tight," Miranda sighed as she glided down Mason's body, wanting to taste her. Her tongue touched Mason for the very first time and slid the length of her as she stroked deeply, feeling Mason's body ripple around her fingers. Fast and hard is what Mason needed and Miranda somehow knew this and drove her completely crazy, her mouth turning her inside out.

"Oh, oh," Mason's moans came from deep inside her chest and she cried out before her body shuddered and then went totally slack on the bed.

Miranda's fingers were still inside Mason, and she kissed her one last time and slowly removed her fingers, drawing another cry from Mason. Completely undone by Miranda's attentions, Mason allowed Miranda to tuck her against her body, holding her securely, a feeling of contentment filling her body for the first time in many years. Miranda's lips slid against Mason's in a kiss that filled Mason's heart with affection for the woman who had just made love to her with so much intensity. It had drained Mason's already exhausted body.

Exhausted or not, Mason wanted to make love to Miranda and nothing short of death would have prevented her. She returned Miranda's kiss as she ran her hands down Miranda's arms and linked fingers with her. Mason's feelings welled up, as she loved Miranda's mouth with her own. Slow, mesmerizing kisses seduced Miranda all over again. Mason's tongue entered Miranda's mouth tasting her, the flavor of her filling Mason completely.

Mason's mouth traveled over Miranda's full breasts and her tongue swirled around and around Miranda's beckoning nipples, deep rose colored and aching to be touched. Mason rolled Miranda on top of her pushing her knees between Miranda's thighs opening her up to Mason's searching fingers. As her mouth suckled heavily on Miranda's nipple, Mason's fingertips slid against Miranda's swollen lips and she slowly entered her. Miranda's head fell onto Mason's shoulder as she was thrown into an orgasm that wracked her body with pleasure.

Mason knew exactly what would please Miranda. She opened her up until her wet center was pressed tightly against Mason's body. Rocking her hips, Mason rolled and bucked against Miranda, her fingers sealed deep inside. Miranda scrambled to her knees as she arched up and tightened her thighs around Mason's hips. Mason sat up and ran her other hand across Miranda's breasts as Miranda rocked hard against Mason's hand. Mason's mouth left moist kisses on her shoulders, neck, and face as Miranda's body trembled with pleasure, her arms locked around Mason's neck. Miranda's head fell back as she gave herself over to Mason's lovemaking, jerking once, twice, and then slumping against Mason, gasping for breath. Mason lay back on the bed, pulling Miranda down with her, folding her arms around her. Miranda's body was soft and tight against Mason's as they lay silent, overwhelmed, and full of new feelings. Mason could have stayed like this for days. Pleasure, affection, and emotion coursed through her body.

"I need to feed you," Miranda whispered against Mason's neck, her lips leaving soft, gentle kisses against her skin.

"Do you have any cereal?"

"I do," Miranda chuckled. "And I probably have milk and toast."

"Then I vote we have a bowl of cereal and climb back into bed," Mason suggested, nuzzling Miranda's neck with her lips. She couldn't seem to stop touching Miranda.

Miranda sighed as Mason played with her neck. "Mason, you aren't going to get cereal any time soon if you keep kissing my neck."

Mason pulled away from Miranda and grinned at her. "Remember where I was."

Miranda stood up with a grin of her own and walked to her dresser drawer to grab a nightshirt for herself and Mason. Mason's eyes stayed on Miranda's incredible body. Her hair was still tucked up in a wavy knot on the back of her head, stray curls hanging down her neck, and Mason felt her heart pound in her chest as Miranda turned to face her.

"You're beautiful," Mason's voice was husky, her eyes locked on Miranda's face.

The comment startled Miranda and she stood motionless, her expression one of surprise and slight embarrassment. "Thank you. Here's a tee shirt to wear while we eat dinner."

"Thanks. Do you mind if I use your bathroom?"

Miranda bent over Mason who lay still on the bed, her lean, naked body relaxed and comfortable. "Mason, you don't have to ask to use anything. The towels and washcloths are clean, and if you need anything else just look around."

Mason reached up and captured a loose curl in her fingers, tugging Miranda close. Her lips brushed softly against Miranda's, drawing a sigh from her as she returned the kiss, her hand gently touching Mason's cheek. They drew the kiss out and felt the passion simmer inside themselves.

"Miranda, can I ask you something?" Mason played with Miranda's fingers while Miranda leaned over her.

"Of course."

"Did you know this would happen?"

Miranda watched Mason carefully, preparing to close her heart while she answered. Here it was: the question about her abilities. "I didn't know when, but when I met you I knew that we would be lovers at some point." Miranda waited for the anger as she met Mason's direct gaze.

"When you read my thoughts earlier, did you really see what I was thinking?" Mason's lips quirked into a slight grin as she remembered thinking about making love to Miranda. The thought hadn't come close to the actual experience.

"You mean the image of you making love to me?" Miranda grinned down at her. "Mason, I won't read your thoughts unless you ask me to. It goes against everything I believe in. I promise."

Mason's smile grew bigger as she pulled Miranda's face close to hers again. "Miranda, can you read my thoughts now?"

"Do you want me to?" Miranda's heart was lost at that moment. She had never been with a woman who touched her soul the way Mason did.

"Miranda, read my thoughts." Mason continued to smile at her.

Miranda slowed her breathing and concentrated on Mason, clearing her head of everything but her. Images flickered in her mind and then she clearly felt the emotion move from Mason to her. It was passion, hunger for her, and the beginnings of love slipping in at the edges. She closed her eyes and pulled the image inside her, warmth filling her heart. Mason's hand slid against her face in a loving gesture, and Miranda opened her eyes and gazed back.

"Mason, if you concentrate you can read my thoughts." Miranda's fingers touched her lips, tracing them slowly.

Mason stared at Miranda as she focused on her with a beaming smile. "We aren't going to be eating dinner any time soon."

Miranda chuckled as her hands found Mason's breasts and stroked them slowly. "See, I told you, you could do it."

Mason laughed as she pulled Miranda down on the bed and ran her hands down her slim back and hips. She wasn't hungry for anything but Miranda. Making love with her was the only thought in her head. She shimmered with feeling as they kissed, and both women felt the connection. Their hearts and bodies had recognized each other.

It was another hour and a half before they sat in the kitchen sharing a bowl of cereal and some toast. Both women had been up a long time, Mason almost twenty hours, Miranda close to eighteen.

"Come on honey, you need some sleep. You must be beat." Miranda touched Mason's arm affectionately.

"I'm not. What about you? You've been up for a long time too."

"I'm fine. Finish your cereal. We're going to bed."

Mason grinned at the gorgeous woman giving her orders while wearing nothing but a tee shirt. "I'm done."

Mason placed the empty bowl in the sink along with Miranda's plate and then, taking Miranda by the hand, she led the way back into the bedroom. They stood in the bathroom together brushing their teeth and chatting comfortably about the little things that two people who lived together might talk about. Within minutes they had stripped their tee shirts off and fallen into Miranda's bed, arms wrapped tightly around each other. After sharing a last slow, delicious kiss, both women slipped almost instantly into sleep.

Mason slept heavily next to Miranda, her fingers twisted possessively in her hair, her arm tucked around her waist. Miranda woke up several hours after they had climbed into bed and turned to watch Mason sleep. She smiled as she saw how peaceful and relaxed Mason looked, her pretty features soft in slumber. Miranda knew she was an intense, serious person when it came to doing her job, but the woman that had touched her earlier with such gentleness was full of passion. Miranda had fallen in love. For the first time in her life, she was in love with a beautiful, talented, Seattle police detective. Miranda snuggled up against Mason and pressed a kiss to her forehead. Mason mumbled in her sleep and tightened her arms around Miranda, tucking her face even closer to Miranda's before settling back into sleep. Miranda's smile lasted long after she, too, had drifted back to sleep.

Chapter 12

▼

The sun shining through the blinds woke Mason and she found Miranda stretched across her body still sleeping. Mason ran her hand slowly down Miranda's back in a loving caress as she watched her sleep. Miranda was so fascinating with her incredible talents and her abiding commitment to children. She was also sexy, gorgeous, and Mason loved touching her, loving her. Something felt so right about being with her. She was surprised that they'd ended up in bed together after just one day, but the frustrations of the day must have fueled their fires. She felt a deep connection with Miranda that she had never experienced before. They had both exploded with lust once they got started, and Mason knew it wasn't a one-time thing. She'd fallen in love with Miranda the moment Miranda had looked at her with tears in her eyes for a wounded young child. Mason had known that when she fell in love it would be with someone special, and Miranda was special indeed. There was something predestined between the two of them and Mason wasn't going to do anything but allow it to happen.

"Good morning." Miranda's eyes opened to find Mason looking at her, her expression one of affection.

"Good morning. How did you sleep?"

"Wonderfully." Miranda captured Mason's face in her hands and pressed her lips to Mason's in a kiss that made every fiber in Mason's body tingle. They shared kiss after kiss, wanting the slow kindling of passion this morning. Fingertips traced across skin that craved to be touched, tongues tasted, and hearts pounded.

Mason rolled Miranda onto her back and covered her breasts and stomach with moist kisses, locking the taste of Miranda's body in her mind. Stroking her hands down Miranda's thighs, Mason wrapped them around her hips as she pressed her wet center hard against Miranda's. Rolling her hips back and forth, Mason and Miranda's bodies intimately connected over and over, their mouths greedily kissing until Mason felt Miranda tremble. Moving her hips faster, she arched her body against Miranda's once, twice, and Miranda cried out in gratification, shivering with feeling. Pleasure like she had never before experienced rolled through Mason as she surrendered to her own needs and moaned before slumping on top of Miranda, undone by her own orgasm. The two of them lay motionless, trying to catch their breath, arms holding each other tight, faces tucked against each other.

Mason turned to Miranda and kissed her slowly, then placed her face tight against Miranda's. "Boy, I've never enjoyed making love like I do with you."

Miranda's chest rumbled with a throaty laugh, her eyes full of humor. "I'm glad you like it."

"That came out all wrong," Mason groaned as she turned so she could see Miranda's face. "I've never felt like this before."

Miranda's fingers touched Mason's face and she smiled. "I feel the same way."

"I don't want to get out of bed, but I need to go to work. I need to see if anyone has found anything in the files that we can follow up on."

Miranda smiled up at the disgruntled woman looking down at her. "I know. Are you going to need me today?"

The sexy smile on Mason's face made Miranda's heart flutter. "I'm going to need you more than today." Mason's hand moved down to encircle her breast.

"I meant at work," Miranda hissed with pleasure.

"Can I call you once I've checked in with my team and see what they've found out?"

"Of course. I'm going to be at work and you have my number."

"Can I see you again, outside of work?" Mason's fingers were slowly massaging Miranda's breast.

"See me?" Miranda chuckled as she kissed Mason.

Mason stopped her attention to Miranda's breast and placed both of her hands on either side of Miranda's face, returning the kiss. "Miranda, I don't just want to sleep with you. I want to get to know you better. I've seen how amazing your gifts are, but I also know you have an incredible heart. I want to spend time with you and see if you and I are more than just a chance meeting. I haven't slept with anyone for a very long time, until you. Making love isn't something I treat casually."

"Mason, I want to keep seeing you, but right now you need to concentrate on finding the little girl and catching this man before he kills her. I'll be here and I certainly want to see you, but I understand completely your priorities."

"I'll catch him, Miranda, but I'm going to need your help. You're also a priority. I want to keep seeing you outside of work."

"Honey, I want to see you."

"Good."

"Let's get up and I'll go make some coffee while you hop in the shower and then call your office."

"Miranda, I more than enjoyed our night together."

"I did too." Miranda kissed her softly. "Go take a shower, honey."

Mason padded to the bathroom and shut the door. Miranda's eyes stayed on her slim, muscular body until the door shut. Mason moved with the grace and strength of an athlete, sexy and appealing. Miranda climbed out of bed and headed for the hall bathroom to clean up before making a pot of coffee for Mason. Twenty minutes later Mason found her wearing her bathrobe, standing silently staring out her kitchen window, lost in thought.

Mason had no choice but to get back into her now wrinkled two-day-old clothes. As she entered the kitchen, she was stopped short as she took in the sight of Miranda serenely looking out her window. She had unpinned her hair and it fell in loose waves down to the middle of her back. Mason's heart swelled with what she now knew was love.

Miranda turned and smiled at her, and Mason's eyes filled with tears. "I can't believe how incredibly beautiful you are."

"Thank you." Miranda was moved. She turned and approached Mason, kissing her softly. Miranda trembled as she felt Mason's emotions move over her in waves. Mason's arms slid around Miranda's waist and they shared another gentle, meaningful kiss.

Several minutes later Miranda broke reluctantly away from Mason and poured two cups of coffee. "Here; I know you need to get going, and I need to get ready for work. I'm just having a hard time letting you go."

"Thanks. I'm having the same problem. I hate to leave you but I have to go to my apartment and get a fresh set of clothes."

"Mason, if you can, can we see each other tonight?"

"I would love to see you later but it depends on how the day goes. I'll tell you what. I'll bring my overnight bag back with me and I'll call you later. If nothing happens in the case, can I come spend the night with you?"

A smile bloomed on Miranda's lips. "I'd love that."

Chapter 13

Thirty minutes later, Mason charged into her apartment and headed for the bedroom. She stripped off her clothes and rifled through her drawers for clean underwear. A short time later, she was fully dressed in a fresh outfit, her overnight bag on her shoulder. As she climbed into her car she dialed her cell phone and connected with her squad.

"Ken, this is Mason; how's it going?"

"Hey, Mason. We've entered all of the data from yesterday's interview notes into the computer. About twenty names came up. Each family is somehow connected to the Pee Wee Tee Ball league. Matt just joined us and those two FBI agents are on their way. We figured you'd want a report first thing this morning on what we found."

"You figured right. I should be there in about twenty minutes."

"We'll be ready."

"Thanks, Ken, I owe you."

"No problem. But you can put in a good word for me with the Chief. My girlfriend is really pissed that I'm still on nights. If I work nights much longer she's going to dump me."

"I'll see what I can do." Mason had spent her own time working the night shift and she knew just how unpopular it could make a person with his or her significant other. Two women had stopped seeing her for just that reason, that and the fact that every time they planned a date something interrupted it. That something was Mason's job.

Twenty minutes later Mason's long strides carried her into the detective squad room, her hands full of a box of Crispy Crème donuts.

"Hey guys."

"Crispies—thanks, Mason." The detectives descended on the box like a starving hoard.

"So what have we got?" She pulled out a chair and sat down next to Matt.

"We've got quite a few names of men that are either directly or indirectly linked to the Pee Wee Tee Ball league. League games are every Saturday at eleven. I was thinking that we could attend a few and observe some of the men. It's a long shot but it's solid. They wouldn't know we were looking at them or have made any connection, so I suggest we don't announce our presence. Everything fits, Mason, the gravel in the shoe, the children not being fearful, and the dark uniform. Maybe he's a coach. Hey, where's Miranda?"

"She's at work. I'll call her if we need her for anything. Are you thinking that she could pick up something from the guy we're looking for if she's there? We could have her walk around and try to get some kind of connection."

"I don't know if she can do that, but it's worth a try. We need to locate this little girl. I couldn't sleep again last night knowing she was still missing."

"I know, Matt. I'll call Miranda and see if she's willing to do it. You know, even if she identifies this guy we won't be able to do anything but follow him. We have nothing that could be used in court." Mason had slept without any thoughts of anyone but Miranda. She felt rested, refreshed, and ready to face another busy day. She felt so good that she thought she could accomplish anything.

"I know, but we have to try something." Matt sighed and looked closely at his partner. "Hey, did you get a haircut or something? You look really nice today."

Mason blushed and shook her head. "No, I didn't get a haircut."

"You really look good. You have a date or something?"

"Cut it out, Matt." Mason stood up and moved back to her desk.

Matt watched his partner carefully. There was something different about Mason. She looked rested and happy, and that was very rare since this case had started. He would figure it out. Mason couldn't keep a secret from him for long.

Mason picked up the telephone to call Miranda. Miranda had just stepped out of the shower, her hair wrapped up in a towel, another towel around her body as she snatched the telephone up to her ear. "Hello."

"What are you doing?"

Miranda smiled as she sat down on the bed. "I just got out of the shower."

"Are you naked?" Mason whispered into her cell phone.

"Mason," Miranda laughed as she felt her body react to Mason's whispered question.

"Good news. We have an opportunity on Saturday to try and get a handle on the man you described from the children's images. Are you still willing to help us?"

"You know I am."

"Would you be able to pick up on this guy if you were around him in a crowd, say at a ball park?"

"I might. It depends on how big the crowd is, if he's there, and whether he's capable of blocking his thoughts. But I'm willing to try."

"Miranda, I don't want to put you in jeopardy, so you're going to be attending the tee ball tournament with one of our undercover cops. I'll explain it all to you later after my team and I figure out all the details. I have to walk it by the Chief before I go any further."

"You think he's going to have a problem with me being involved?"

"Not when I explain everything to him." Mason tried to sound positive but she knew she was in for a fight. "I'll call you later and let you know what's going on."

"Mason, I only have appointments for the morning, and I planned to work on my files this afternoon. If you need me to come in, just call."

"I will. Miranda, I already miss you." Mason's voice was low and laden with emotion.

"I miss you too, honey."

"Goodbye."

Miranda hung up the telephone and sat on the bed considering the last eventful day. She had a good hour before she had to get ready for work. She needed to call her mom. She needed to talk to her about Mason, the case, and her heart—especially her heart. She, her mother, and grandmother were very close and they stayed connected both by telephone and by thought.

Chapter 14

When Miranda's life as a child had gotten a bit rough, due to her talents or her mother's notoriety, it was her grandmother who would become furious. She loved her granddaughter ferociously, her family was worth protecting, and she had no patience for people who were, in her own words, *idiots*! Her grandmother's emotions ran deep and strong. Her grandmother was also one of the most outrageous people one could ever hope to meet. Rose O'Malley didn't care what people thought of her. She was proud of who she was and even prouder of her gracious and beautiful daughter and granddaughter. No one hurt her family and got away with it. She was one of a kind and deeply loved by both her daughter and granddaughter.

Rose had grown up hiding her own psychic abilities as she had been taught to do by her own mother. In Ireland, people were a little more understanding of special talents but, as a young child, Rose and her family had fled to the United States looking for more opportunities. They had settled in New Orleans not only because Rose's father was a talented furniture maker but to protect his special family. He felt the more open and diverse culture there would be safer for his wife and daughter.

Rose's childhood had been full of happiness, openness, and love. The French Quarter furniture shop had grown with her father's success, and Rose and her mother were absorbed into the culture. The small but supportive community in the French Quarter accepted their psychic abilities, and Rose rarely had to deal with prejudice and stupidity.

It broke her heart that her only daughter was treated differently than the other children. But Rose raised her daughter judiciously, and despite some minor discrimination, she grew to be a beautiful, sensible woman. In turn, her daughter had raised a daughter of her own. Rose couldn't have been prouder of Miranda and woe to the person who would hurt her granddaughter.

The most painful time for both Rose and Miranda's mother, Moira, was when Miranda attended college. No one had been surprised by Miranda's declaration in high school that she was a lesbian. There had been numerous signs, and Moira loved her daughter unconditionally. It was Miranda's first real relationship that worried both her mother and Rose. Miranda had fallen in love with a woman who wanted to be a journalist. There was a ruthlessness to the woman that Miranda had ignored in the haziness of falling in love for the first time. But Rose and Moira saw it and it bothered them. Miranda was adamant about not using her talents when it came to her personal relationships. She knew she could open herself up and look into her new girlfriend's heart, but she refused to do so. She also cautioned her mother, and most particularly her grandmother, not to look either. It was important to her that her relationship with Suzanne be open and honest, without interference.

Of course, Rose had ignored her granddaughter and looked anyway. What she saw broke her heart, and there was absolutely nothing she could do about it. Her daughter had known Rose would look, but she had dragged a promise from her that she would not meddle, and a promise was a promise. Rose and Moira stood by and watched as Miranda's heart was utterly broken and, more importantly, her confidence in herself shaken, something that infuriated Rose more than anything else. To her, her granddaughter was as close to perfect as a person could get.

Suzanne had been with Miranda for only one reason, and that reason was not for love. Not that sleeping with Miranda had been a hardship. The whole time she was with her, she was writing an exposé on the life of a woman psychic. Suzanne wanted to jump-start her career as a reporter and, after hawking the idea to a tabloid, she had systematically recorded everything that she learned about Miranda and her family's psychic abilities. Miranda had shared everything with Suzanne—her body, her heart, and her family. She had no idea that everything she shared with Suzanne would end up in a series of articles in a newspaper. Because she was in love and thought the feeling was reciprocated, she answered every one of Suzanne's questions honestly and openly. Wasn't that what you did when you were in a relationship? She hadn't noticed that Suzanne was spending less and less time with her. Miranda had assumed it was because of their class loads. But Suzanne had gotten everything she wanted from her unsuspecting lover.

The day that Suzanne's first installment appeared in the tabloid, Miranda had attended her psychology class. A young man approached and asked her to autograph his copy of the article. She hadn't seen Suzanne for a couple of days, but it was normal for them to be apart for at least a two or three days each week. She had taken the paper from him in confusion, reading it in front of all her classmates. What she had read destroyed her. She was numb with shock and hurt so deep that she felt her heart break. She held her emotions and shock inside until she got away from class and fled to her apartment. Devastated and hurting, Miranda waited for an explanation from Suzanne. For five hours Miranda cried as she called Suzanne's number over and over again. Finally she realized that Suzanne would not be coming back. She'd gotten exactly what she wanted from Miranda—a story and instant notoriety.

Moira found her heartbroken daughter sobbing in her bedroom and gathered her in her arms, holding her tightly. No words of comfort could heal the deep wounds that lodged in Miranda's heart.

"I loved her, Mom," Miranda cried, her eyes red-rimmed, her voice hoarse. But it was her heart that Moira was most worried about. For the first time in her life, Miranda had given hers away, and Suzanne had trampled on that gift. Moira was terribly concerned that her daughter would close herself off to love, and that would be a terribly lonely existence.

"I know you did." And she held her daughter and cried with her. Miranda survived her crushing heartbreak by immediately going back to school and responding to the curious glances and sometimes-hurtful remarks with humor and grace. Moira and Rose were extremely proud of her. Not that Rose hadn't wanted Suzanne's blood; she ranted and raved for weeks to her daughter, threatening to curse Suzanne for the rest of her life.

"Hi, Mom."

"Miranda, I was just going to call you. Talk to me, honey. What's going on? I feel a dark disturbance around you."

"I'm helping the police find a little girl who was kidnapped yesterday. It's the third child he's taken."

"Have you connected with him?"

"Not yet."

"Be very careful, Miranda. Evil like that is more than destructive." Moira knew firsthand. She'd helped in several cases over the years. She had spent many horrifying moments balanced on the slender bridge between sanity and madness, as she had connected with inhuman monsters that committed unspeakable atrocities. "Are you okay, honey?"

"So far I'm okay. The children are so damaged, Mom. It breaks my heart. They're in so much pain. I'm not sure if I can help them very much."

"Do you need my help?"

"You can't get here in time, and I'm okay for now."

"Honey, what else is going on?"

"I met someone."

Those three words were cause for Moira to rejoice. She didn't have to be told that this was her daughter's soul mate. She knew, and it made her unbelievably happy.

Miranda's mother smiled as she recognized the emotion in her daughter's voice. She knew this relationship was special. "Who is she?"

"The detective in charge of the case. Her name is Mason. Mom, I'm in love with her."

"How does she feel about you?"

"I think she has affection for me and is capable of loving me."

"But..."

"I know she's going to be put to a test, and it's going to require her to trust in my abilities."

"And you don't know if she will?"

"I won't look. Mom, I don't want to find out that way."

Miranda's mother knew her daughter well. "Honey, if she's the one, she'll put her trust in you."

"I know. I really think she's the one."

"Then I want to meet her."

"Are you coming for a visit soon?"

"Maybe, honey. Mama wants to see her granddaughter, and I need to see my beautiful girl."

"How is Grandma?"

"Just as ornery as ever. She said something this morning about putting a curse on the gardener. He's trying to convince her to plant roses in the back yard."

Miranda giggled at her mother's comment. Miranda's grandmother was always threatening to curse someone, and she hated roses. She didn't want a plant with her name in the yard. "I would love to see you both. Come soon, Mom."

"Love you, and honey, just be yourself. No one can resist a beautiful, smart woman who has a loving and generous heart."

Miranda smiled as she placed the telephone on her nightstand. After her father had died of a heart attack four years earlier, the three women were all that was left of their family, and they remained very close. She would like her grandmother to meet Mason. She thought Mason could hold her own with the unique woman. She grinned as she thought about their interaction. It would be very interesting.

Chapter 15

"A what?" The Chief of Detective's voice thundered through his office. He was furious, white hot angry, and it was all directed at his lead detective. His eyes flashed and his face darkened as he rose out of his chair and towered over Mason.

"She's a psychologist and a psychic." Mason flushed but she wouldn't back down. She had to convince him that the plan would work. She had no doubt that Miranda was the key to cracking the case. "She was instrumental in our making a connection to the Pee Wee Tee Ball league. It makes sense, Chief. He's taking kids that he comes in contact with. He gets to know them so they aren't afraid. They go willingly with him."

"Goddamn it, Mason, a psychic! What were you thinking?" The Chief was not convinced that Mason's plan was sound.

"Boss, she was able to get a description from both children and she's worked with the FBI before. She's been instrumental in helping them solve several cases. The team is sure about this lead, Chief."

"Let me see if I understand you. You want to send her with an undercover to the ball field where she will—what did you say?—*Scan the field for the perp?*"

Mason didn't have to be told what the Chief thought of the idea. If his tone didn't indicate that he was unconvinced, the incredulous look on his face was a clear marker of his feelings. "Chief, this guy stalks the kids at the playfield. He thinks he's invincible, and he doesn't know we've made the connection. We want to send Dennis and Miranda in looking like parents. No one will know what we're doing. They'll be wired, and we'll monitor them. If we locate him, we'll follow him in hopes that he'll lead us to the missing little girl."

The Chief had to give Mason credit. She and her team had thought of everything; everything, that is, except for the nonsensical idea of using a psychic, or whatever the hell she was! "Mason, I don't like this one bit."

"Chief, we don't have anything else to go on. He's out there and we need to catch him. I don't care what it takes as long as it's legal. I'm going to find that little girl." Mason knew this was the right thing to do. "I'll stake my job on this psychic. She's going to find him; I know it."

"My best detective is putting her job on the line for a psychic. You'd better know what you're doing because if this operation blows up in our faces, your job won't be the only one on the line." The Chief's eyes bored through Mason. The fact that she was placing her job in jeopardy was the deciding factor. He knew his detective's work, and she was his best.

Mason knew when to keep quiet. She waited silently while the Chief made his decision. "I'll let you go ahead with this on one condition."

Mason knew he would have one. She waited patiently to see just what he would demand. "You keep this operation quiet. No one is to talk about it to anyone. If nothing comes of it, we write it up as a failed surveillance based on a tip, no psychics in the report."

"Okay, I can do that."

"And Mason, you had better be right about this or you and I are going to have a serious talk about your job future." Chief Marston wouldn't fire his detective, but he could make her sweat for making a bad decision.

"Yes, Chief." She stood up and high-tailed it out of his office. It wasn't smart to hang around the Chief when he was pissed, and he was still royally mad. She headed to the conference room where her team waited.

"So is it a go?"

"Yes, we've been given the go-ahead with a couple of conditions. We're on a *need to know* about this operation. Guys, it's very important that we don't talk about this to anyone on the outside. The Chief is extremely unhappy that I brought a psychic in. Now, let's review the plan and make sure we've got our asses covered."

"Okay, Mason. Are you going to have Miranda come in this evening?"

"No; Dennis can meet me at Miranda's tomorrow morning, and he can take her to the ball field. She doesn't need to be involved in the preplanning."

"She's agreed to this?"

"Yes, she's perfectly comfortable with the plan."

"Will connecting to a freak like this hurt Miranda?" Matt asked. The team waited expectantly for Mason's response. None of them wanted to put Miranda in jeopardy.

"I don't know. She obviously felt every bit of pain that the children felt. I don't know what will happen. But Dennis, if at any time you think Miranda is in pain or danger of being harmed, I want you to pull the plug."

Mason would never forget watching Miranda interview the children. Knowing that she could feel everything the children had been subjected to made Mason's heart ache, for the children and for her new lover. She knew without a doubt that Miranda hadn't thought once about herself as she helped the children. This, more than anything, made Mason want to protect her.

"I will, Mason," Dennis agreed, as he sat up in his chair. "What's Miranda like?"

Mason felt her heart flutter in her chest as she prepared to respond, but Matt beat Mason with an answer. "She's beautiful, loving, very gentle, and extremely talented. She's special. You just know it when you're around her. No one can spend any time around her and not feel it."

"Is she single?"

"Dennis, Miranda is not to be hit on. She's doing this as a favor, and I want us to treat her with professionalism." Mason felt jealousy well up and almost overwhelm her. Dennis better not make a move on Miranda!

Dennis grinned at Mason. He wouldn't have done anything, but he couldn't help but ask Mason. She seemed a little uptight about the operation. "I promise I won't kiss on her."

Mason couldn't keep from grinning at Dennis. He was a good looking man, but what he didn't know was that Miranda had eyes only for Mason, and that couldn't have pleased Mason more. "Okay guys, let's get to work."

Two hours later Mason rang Miranda's buzzer and waited to be let upstairs. It was after seven. She had stayed until the last of the details had been buttoned down before she left. She couldn't afford any slipups. A young girl was still missing. She also had another worry. She didn't want to put Miranda in a situation that was dangerous. She entered the elevator with her overnight bag on her shoulder. For one night she was going to forget work and just enjoy an evening with a beautiful woman. Miranda had convinced Mason to let her fix dinner. All Mason had to do was show up. Mason was doing a little bit more than showing up. She held a long stemmed pale pink rose, and she simmered with feeling as she exited the elevator. Miranda stood just outside the open door of her condo, a welcoming smile on her face.

"Hello, Detective."

"Hi. You look wonderful." Mason handed the rose to Miranda as she stared at her long, colorful skirt, a loose, cobalt blue blouse, and bare feet.

"What a pretty rose; thank you."

Miranda turned to let her in the condo, but Mason reached out and snagged her with her arm, gently pulling her up against her. "I missed you so much."

It wasn't the rose or the words that made Miranda's heart tremble, it was the gentle kiss that told her Mason meant what she said. Gently she loved Miranda with her mouth as Miranda's arms slipped around Mason and hugged her tightly.

"We'd better go inside," Miranda whispered against Mason's lips unwilling to let her go for even an instant. "Dinner is just about ready."

Mason followed Miranda into the tastefully appointed condo and again moved up to the huge window and the compelling landscape outside. "I can't get over how soothing this view is. Being here with you makes me feel so relaxed and safe. It's like I belong here."

"You do belong here," Miranda promised as she took the overnight bag from Mason's shoulder. "I'll put your bag in the other room. There's an open bottle of wine on the kitchen counter; would you pour us both a glass?"

"Of course; I appreciate your fixing dinner, but I wanted to take you out."

Miranda turned and smiled at Mason as she headed down the hall. "Honey, I didn't want to go out where I'd have to keep my hands off you. I thought that was a good enough reason to eat here."

Mason grinned at Miranda and watched her walk down the hall to the bedroom before she turned into the kitchen. She poured them both a glass of wine and then took off her jacket so she could remove her shoulder harness. Some women were bothered by Mason's wearing a firearm. She hung the weapon on a chair under her jacket trying to disguise the fact that she carried a loaded gun.

Miranda slipped up behind her and hugged her tightly. "Would you like to hang your gun in the closet?"

"If you don't mind?" Mason was worried that Miranda was disturbed about her carrying a gun.

"Honey, I don't mind you doing anything in my home. Your gun doesn't bother me. It's a part of who you are."

Miranda hugged Mason tightly, just wanting to hold her all night. "I could hold you for hours."

Miranda's smile was immense as she looked up at the woman she was madly in love with. "I would love to hold you all night, but you need to eat. You've been working for twelve hours."

The two women enjoyed a leisurely dinner. Miranda had prepared a veal scaloppini and crisp, tender asparagus spears, accompanied by a nice glass of white wine. Mason couldn't remember the last time she had enjoyed a home cooked meal.

They visited quietly, neither one mentioning the next day's activities. It was an evening of romance, full of mutual attraction, as they shared stories of their lives. It was after ten before they had cleaned up the kitchen and sat in the living room enjoying the sparkling night time view. Mason's arm was around Miranda who sat with her legs underneath her, leaning against Mason. Mason played with Miranda's hair that was pinned up on top of her head. Mason wanted to see it loose and flowing.

"Miranda, can I take the pins out of your hair?"

Miranda turned and looked at Mason with a half smile. "I can unpin it."

"Let me, please?"

Miranda watched Mason's face as Mason slowly removed a pin. A length of Miranda's chestnut hair fell in waves down her back. Mason's smile made Miranda shiver as she sat still enjoying Mason's total involvement in her task. It took Mason almost ten minutes to unpin Miranda's hair and by then Miranda was ready to explode. She wanted to kiss Mason desperately.

Mason gathered Miranda's hair up in her hands and bent over putting her face against it. "Your hair is so beautiful, all sorts of browns and gold all mixed together, and the scent is you. I love the way you smell, elegant and sexy. I just want to bury my face in it all night."

Miranda caught her breath as Mason's lips slid against her neck tasting the skin behind her ear. Miranda sighed as she wrapped her arms around Mason's neck. Mason's lips covered Miranda's face with soft kisses, touching everywhere but her lips, and Miranda trembled.

"Mason, please kiss me."

Mason fingers traced Miranda's face as she leaned closer, her blue eyes locked onto Miranda's green ones. Their breaths mingled and then their lips, as Mason loved Miranda with her mouth. Over and over they kissed. Mason was in no hurry as she stroked Miranda's back and shoulders. Miranda's hands shook as she reached up and slid her fingers through Mason's blond hair and held her face as she smiled up at her.

"I love how you kiss me."

Mason smiled down at her and reached up and clasped her hand with her fingers. Turning it over, she kissed Miranda's palm. Miranda felt need well up inside herself, and she was through waiting. Her fingers went to the buttons of Mason's silk blouse. Mason didn't move as Miranda took her time unbuttoning every button until Mason's shirt lay open. Miranda's eyes traveled lower. She saw Mason's snowy white lace bra and the full breasts that all but overflowed it. She bent and kissed Mason's cleavage and ran her tongue slowly over her skin. She kissed Mason's breast and then nuzzled her nipple through the lace. Miranda's attentions made Mason groan. Miranda's mouth covered both nipples over and over until Mason thought she'd go crazy.

"Miranda, can we move this into the bedroom?" she gasped as Miranda's tongue touched her stomach.

"Let's."

Miranda stood up and reached down to clasp Mason's hand and tugged her up. They moved down the hall with Mason's hand in hers. She entered the bedroom and turned to face Mason, her eyes glowing in the dimly lit room.

"I can't believe how much I want you."

"As much as I want you."

Miranda's hands clasped Mason's wrists, lowering Mason slowly onto the bed, stretching her arms over her head. "Don't move. I'm going to take all your clothes off."

Miranda's fingers worked quickly. First, she removed Mason's shirt, then her bra, followed by her slacks, nylons, and underwear until she was totally naked. Miranda's eyes traveled the length of Mason's body, admiring the healthy, feminine strength that was all Mason. "I love your body."

Mason smiled up at Miranda. "Are you going to take your clothes off?"

"Oh, yeah, and I'm going to let you watch me." Miranda's comment turned Mason inside out, and she started to sit up.

"No, you're going to lay there and not move."

"But I want to touch you."

"You'll get the chance." Miranda slowly began to unbutton her blouse as she grinned down at Mason. She had never stripped for anyone before, but she knew Mason would enjoy watching her disrobe.

Mason's eyes never left Miranda. She watched Miranda take off her blouse and bra. Her skirt dropped to the floor, and Mason saw the thong underwear. She moaned again. "You're killing me, Miranda. Your underwear makes me want to bury my face between your legs."

"That sounds delicious, but my turn first." Miranda laughed as she dropped her underwear to the floor and slowly covered Mason's naked body with her own.

Miranda's mouth met Mason's in a kiss that rocked them both. Mason's hands slid down over Miranda's taut buttocks. Miranda felt the heat begin as their fingertips once again memorized every part of each other's body. The room was filled with sighs of pleasure as both of them succumbed to lovemaking that touched their very souls.

Mason's fingertips barely skimmed Miranda's slick center, but it was enough to turn Miranda inside out. Miranda's hand worked its way between Mason's thighs and entered her swiftly as Mason cried out in pleasure. Mason's fingers filled Miranda completely and they stroked each other over and over until both women reached shattering orgasms. Mason's face lay buried in Miranda's hair, her lips touching her cheek as she tried to catch her breath. Miranda lay on top of Mason, too overwhelmed to move. Mason reached down and clasped Miranda's fingers with her own.

Miranda felt love for Mason ripple through her body, and she lay quietly enjoying their closeness. Mason's lips touched Miranda's mouth lightly and she sighed as she looked up at Miranda.

"Every time we make love, it's more."

Miranda started to move off of Mason's body but Mason quickly protested. "Please stay. I love the feel of you lying on me."

"I'll stay here all night if you want."

Mason's eyes began to droop with exhaustion as the last couple of weeks with little sleep and lots of stress took their toll. Miranda reached down and pulled the covers up over them and kissed Mason gently.

"Go to sleep, honey."

"I need to hold you."

"All night, sweetie, I promise." Miranda rolled to Mason's side and hugged her. "Please get some sleep."

"Miranda, I…"

"Go to sleep, honey."

Mason had almost admitted to Miranda that she was in love with her as she drifted slowly into slumber. She needed to tell her soon. She wanted Miranda in her life for a long, long time. Miranda didn't need to be told that Mason loved her. She knew by the way Mason held her, the way she touched her and looked at her with such naked emotion. Mason held nothing back in her lovemaking and her feelings. Miranda slipped into a contented sleep, her arms tightly around Mason, her face tucked against the back of her shoulder.

Chapter 16

"Miranda, I've got to go check in with my team. Are you sure you have no questions?"

"None. But I'd like to have another kiss before you go."

"Of course, honey."

Mason gathered Miranda to her and kissed her slowly, savoring the pleasure she got every time she and Miranda came close. Miranda sighed against Mason's mouth. She, too, was overwhelmed by the feelings that welled up inside her body and her heart. Mason and Miranda stood in each other's arms for several moments enjoying the closeness they felt when they were together.

"I have to go."

"I know." Miranda hugged Mason once more and walked with her to the door.

"Dennis will be here around ten-thirty. Just wear anything comfortable for sitting on the bleachers and walking around the ball fields at Lower Woodland Park. Dennis is a very good undercover cop. He knows what he's doing. He'll keep you safe. You're supposed to look like a young married couple watching their child play ball. That cover should give you and Dennis the opportunity to scan the crowd and identify any men you think fit our description. We'll follow up on anything that you and Dennis discover. You'll both be wired so we can hear everything you say."

"Where will you be while I'm at the field?"

"I'm going to be in the monitoring van several blocks away. You both will be able to talk to me through the microphones hidden in your clothing, so I can be there immediately if you need me."

"I'll be ready."

"Miranda, I'll be monitoring you at all times. I don't want to put you in any jeopardy. You and Dennis can call it off at any time. I won't let anything happen to you." Mason's eyes were serious as she met Miranda's eyes.

Miranda smiled back at her. "I know you won't. I trust you, Mason. Be safe."

"I'll see you later." One last gentle kiss and Mason was gone. Miranda was still smiling as she went to shower and get dressed. She had several hours before her partner for the day would arrive, and Miranda wanted to get some work done. Mason was coming back over tonight and they were going to a recently released movie at the neighborhood theater. Life couldn't be better.

Right at ten-thirty, Dennis Mayer rang the bell. Miranda invited him upstairs after he told her Mason was with him. She paced restlessly waiting for them to come up. A quick knock on the door made her jump. Mason was standing next to a very tall blond man who grinned as Miranda opened the door.

"So, you're going to be my wife," he commented with a wink, as he followed Mason into the condo. "Boy, am I a lucky stiff."

"Dennis, quit teasing her," Mason chastised him as she smiled at Miranda. "I can't stay long because we need to get in position at the park, but I wanted to make sure that you're still okay with this."

"I'm fine." Miranda found it difficult to look at Mason without giving away her feelings for her. Mason was wearing a pair of cream-colored slacks, a white blouse, and a loose fitting navy blazer with the sleeves rolled up. Her hair was loose and hung straight to her shoulders. She looked professional, gorgeous, and downright sexy.

"Dennis why don't you go wait in the car? Miranda and I will meet you downstairs in a few minutes."

Dennis grinned at the two women, dimples winking in both cheeks as he turned and headed out of the condominium. Mason waited until the door shut behind him before moving up to Miranda and wrapping her arms around her. "I'll be right there, honey. I'll be close by."

"I'm glad you stopped by." Miranda hugged Mason tightly, breathing in the scent of the woman she loved more than life itself.

"So am I." Mason kissed her slowly, deliciously, and with as much passion as they'd felt the night before. "Miranda, we have to go. Here's the mike and cell phone unit. You need to leave it on the whole time you're there so I can hear everything. If you see or feel anything, let Dennis know—and me."

"I will."

"Most importantly, I need you to be careful. I don't want anything to happen to you."

"You'll make sure nothing happens."

"Come on, honey." Mason held Miranda's hand until she opened the door, squeezing her fingers once before walking down the hall with Miranda. "You look very cute, by the way," Mason commented, taking in Miranda's slim shape nicely defined by faded denim jeans, a purple polo shirt, and a white sweat shirt draped around her shoulders,

Miranda smiled at Mason before replying. "You look beautiful and so professional with your badge on your hip."

Mason's cocky grin made Miranda chuckle. "Miranda, Dennis knows what you're going to be doing and he's probably going to ask you a lot of questions. Explain to him as much as you need to. If at any time you feel the least little bit uncomfortable, let him know."

"You told him I'm a psychic?"

"I did. I had to tell everyone on the team and my boss needed to give the go ahead for this. I needed to explain our plan to him in detail."

"You told your boss?"

"I had to; I hope that was okay."

"What did your boss say?"

"He was skeptical, to say the least, but he's willing to do anything at this point to stop this creep." She decided to keep his opinion of psychics to herself.

The two women walked through the front door of the building and found Dennis standing next to a big, dark green SUV, smoking a cigarette. He grinned at them as he ground the cigarette butt out on the ground.

"Dennis, reacquaint yourself with your wife for the day. Miranda, your husband is waiting for you." Mason smirked as she spoke.

"You ready for this?"

"As ready as I'll ever be."

"So, Miranda, Mason tells me you're a psychic. How's it work?" Dennis looked so interested and sincere that Miranda smiled up at him. She could see immediately why he was good at his job. He was completely disarming.

"Dennis, why don't you let Miranda explain it to you while you're driving to the park? Now remember, you're a married couple that might be watching their kid play tee ball. Wander around from game to game, sit on the bleachers for a while, and just pay attention to all the men you see. Dennis, you've seen our sketches, and Miranda, you'll try to sense whether he's there or not."

"Okay."

"The games are over around three-thirty or four. If we haven't seen anything by then, I'd like you to come back to the squad to record your observations."

"We'll be there."

Mason climbed into her car and waited until Miranda got into the SUV with Dennis. She sighed as she pulled out behind them. Her feelings for Miranda were bubbling inside her, and she had to do her best to force them into the background so she could pay attention to business. The woman was so damn beautiful, and she never once questioned helping with this nasty assignment. She had captured Mason's heart completely. Mason wanted to wrap this case up quickly and put this animal behind bars. She wanted time to be with Miranda and to have a more balanced life.

Mason turned off three blocks from the baseball park and pulled up behind a nondescript van parked in front of a house on a side street. Mason and Matt had spoken to the owners and advised them they were going to be parked out in front for most of the afternoon. Mason climbed into the van while Matt and a young policewoman were testing the recording equipment with Miranda and Dennis. "You're good to go. Take good care of her, Dennis," Matt requested. He liked Miranda very much, and he didn't want her to be placed in any danger.

"Okay, honey. Take my hand and let's look the part." Dennis grinned at Miranda as he held her door open. "I promised Mason I wouldn't try to kiss you."

"I appreciate that, Dennis." Miranda grinned up at him as they strolled to the fields. Matt couldn't help but laugh when Mason rudely snorted at Dennis's comment.

Miranda had explained to Dennis how she was going to try and receive images from the men that fit the profile that had been worked up. He had been amazed at the description of her abilities—and a little skeptical.

"Hey, if Mason believes you can do this, then so do I. Mason is the best detective I know."

Matt slugged Mason in the arm as they listened to the conversation, grinning from ear to ear. Mason wasn't one to take compliments comfortably, so when she received one, Matt made sure she took note of it.

For about twenty minutes, Miranda and Dennis wandered around the baseball diamonds chatting idly as they tried to get a fix on the people that were there. There were four fields in all, and they strolled the gravel paths behind the backstops of each of them.

"Dennis, let's go sit on those bleachers over there. I see three men that might fit the picture."

"Alright." Dennis helped Miranda to a seat on the bleachers and climbed up beside her. He paid attention to the game, clapping and cheering the children on, while Miranda slowed her breathing and centered herself. She scanned each of the men's thoughts in turn. None of them was thinking of anything besides the performance of his child in the game, and Miranda knew that the man they were looking for wasn't there. His thoughts would be chaotic and not full of love for the children around them.

The park was full of excited children and their parents as they practiced the game of baseball. There were tiny children barely able to swing the bat and older youngsters who were showing the skills of budding athletes. The four baseball fields were full of activity as players raced out to their positions and back again to the dugouts. There were little girls who stood in the outfield and played with their shoelaces, and little boys who ran the wrong way when they finally connected with the ball at home plate. Patient coaches and parents grinned and laughed at the foibles of the young, energetic would-be athletes. Dennis and Miranda burst into laughter many times as they watched game after game. If the two of them hadn't been focused on their reason for being there, it would have been a pleasant way to spend a warm, spring day.

For almost five hours, Miranda and Dennis took turns sitting on the bleachers and walking among the crowds. They took a couple of bathroom breaks and made two trips to the concession stand. Dennis and Miranda were striking out. Both were getting tired and very disappointed that not one man had stood out to Miranda or Dennis. The games were winding down, and Miranda and Dennis were standing by the fence watching parents collect their children before returning to their own car.

Miranda's eyes filled with tears as she saw the happy faces of all the cute kids who had no clue that a monster might be stalking them. She started to turn to Dennis, who stood with his arm loosely around her, when she gasped, as black, horrifying images entered her mind. He was there!

"Dennis, he's here!" Miranda hissed, as she searched about for the man that was even now fantasizing about torturing a child. Ghastly images slammed against Miranda's mind making her nauseous. She scanned the quickly diminishing crowd as Dennis signaled to Mason and the team that Miranda had connected with the suspect. While the team got into place to follow him, Miranda fought the nausea she felt and tried to pinpoint his location. The plan was to follow him hoping he would lead them to the location of the missing child.

Miranda's connection was so strong she was frightened that he knew she was there and that he was sending these particularly black thoughts her way. There was no man who matched the sketch or the description that Miranda had gotten from the children's images. Her eyes darted everywhere trying to determine where the dark images were coming from. Dennis stayed glued to Miranda's side, his eyes casting about as he also tried to locate the man that was terrifying Miranda. She was white with fear, her hand clammy, as Dennis held tightly to it. He knew she wasn't faking anything. Her body trembled as she tried to concentrate and not lose the connection.

"Hey, coach, nice job."

"Hey, honey, did you just get here?" A young woman with a baseball cap on her head carried a large bag of equipment over to a man who stood at the end of the bleachers.

Miranda gasped when she saw him. He was a police officer in a blue uniform, a navy blue uniform! No wonder the kids went to him. He was someone they were taught to trust. His hair was short, he wore dark sunglasses, but what was different was the stubble of a beard and moustache. He wasn't the clean-shaven image that the children had locked in their thoughts.

"I just got off. Are you all done?"

"Yes, sweetie, we lost."

"I'm sorry, but you'll get 'em next time. Here, let me carry the equipment."

The woman reached up and tugged his face down to hers. "I love your beard."

"It will fill in pretty quickly. I needed a change." He exchanged a kiss with the young woman.

"Are you going to follow me home?"

"I've got to take care of a few things at my place. I thought I could meet you at the house in about an hour or so. We can go out for pizza and a movie."

"Sounds perfect. I'll have a chance to clean up. Why don't you go ahead and do what you need to do. I need to talk to a couple of parents."

The man that Miranda was concentrating on bent over and kissed the young woman again. He placed the bag of equipment on the ground next to a car in the parking lot and turned to leave.

"Dennis, it's him, the police officer," she whispered, frantic that he would get away before they could follow him. Her eyes never left him as he walked through the crowd.

"You're sure?" Miranda looked up at Dennis and he knew she told the truth. Speaking quietly into his mike, Dennis relayed the information. "He's a police officer, and he's heading for the south end of the parking lot right now. He's not clean-shaven like the sketch. He's growing a beard. He's about six-feet, maybe a little taller. He's wearing dark glasses and a Seattle patrolman's uniform."

"Copy that. We'll follow him. You find out what you can."

"Will do. Can someone come get Miranda? She's pretty shaken up."

"As soon as the suspect is on the move, I'll pick her up."

"Miranda, Mason will be here soon. Can you hold on a little longer?" Dennis was extremely concerned about her. She was breathing shallowly, her face still white with fear. He held her tightly against him as she shook violently.

"I'll be okay. Find out who he is. We need to find the little girl." Miranda breathed in deeply trying to cleanse her mind of the images she had seen of tortured and abused children. It couldn't have been any worse if she had been standing right next to him as he hurt these children. His oily blackness caused her excruciating pain and suffering. The more he hurt them, the more he craved. He was evil personified, and Miranda knew he had to be stopped. His corrupt mind was full of death and destruction.

"Stay right with me." Dennis held tightly to Miranda's hand as he approached the woman coach, a smile on his face. "Excuse me, ma'am?"

"Yes?" The woman coach turned to Dennis and Miranda, a questioning look on her face.

"Was that police officer your husband? He looks like a guy named Rick Senders that I went to high school with." Dennis beamed a huge smile at the woman as he rubbed Miranda's back affectionately.

"He's my boyfriend. His name is Phil Randolph, not Rick."

"I'm sorry; I could swear I know him." Dennis flashed his dimples at her. "I was telling my wife, Miranda, that he was my old buddy."

"No problem; maybe you've seen him while he's on the job or here at the field. Usually he helps me coach on Saturdays. He loves the kids and the kids love him. That's how we met. He was here watching the games one Saturday and we started to talk. We've been seeing each other ever since." The woman relaxed and became talkative as Miranda tried to calm herself long enough to get into her thoughts.

"That's a wonderful story. Miranda and I met at work, didn't we honey?"

Miranda managed a wan smile for the young woman. "Yes."

"We've been married a year and are thinking about having a baby. We like to come watch the kids play tee ball." Dennis grinned at Miranda taking her hand in his. He was trying to keep most of the attention on himself. Miranda was too pale and her eyes were glassy. If someone looked critically at her, they would see that something was wrong.

"That's so sweet. That's just what Phil said. He loves watching children."

"How long have you been dating?"

"About three months, but it feels like we've known each other forever."

Miranda had connected with the young woman's thoughts and knew that her feelings were genuine and ran deep. She was in love with the man called Phil, and was hoping to marry him. Miranda felt sick to her stomach at the thought that such a depraved individual had touched the pleasant young woman. It would break her heart when she found out her new boyfriend had been using her to gain access to young children. She shuddered and looked up into Dennis' eyes with such compassion that he pulled her to him and slipped an arm around her shoulders.

"Well, my wife and I should let you go. What was your name?"

"Sue March."

"I'm Dennis. Thanks very much for your time." Dennis again flashed the woman a warm smile.

"You're welcome."

Dennis steered Miranda toward the parking lot where he could see Mason sitting in her car watching them. He didn't approach her car but continued on to his SUV. "Mason, did you get all that?"

"Yes, and we have two unmarked cars following her home. We have four on the suspect."

"Good. I'm going to take Miranda home. You can get her report later. She's very pale, and I'm a little worried about her." Dennis almost carried Miranda to his vehicle, his voice conveying his concern. "She needs help, Mason."

"I'm fine," Miranda protested as her stomach churned. She had to work hard to keep from vomiting.

"I'll follow you," Mason responded, her voice fraught with worry. There was no telling what Miranda had felt when she connected with the monster. Mason ground her teeth and gripped the steering wheel to keep from exploding. Jesus, what had she done? She shouldn't have used Miranda; now it was too late!

Dennis had Miranda back at her condominium within twenty minutes and was ushering her into the building when Mason pulled up. "Miranda, are you okay?"

"I'm fine," she protested. But she wasn't fine. She was going to be sick.

"Let's get you into your place where you can lay down." Mason supported her left side as Dennis steered her into the building.

Miranda held on until she opened her door and then rushed to the closest bathroom. She could no longer control the heaving of her stomach. Over and over, Miranda vomited until she had nothing left in her stomach. Mason had pushed her way into the bathroom and was holding Miranda's hair back while rubbing her neck. She couldn't think of anything else to do. She was very worried about Miranda and the ache in her chest as she watched her suffer scared her. Dennis stood helplessly in Miranda's living room listening to Miranda's distress.

"Jesus, I need a cigarette!" he muttered, as he paced back and forth.

"I'm okay, now," Miranda whispered, straightening up. "Let me get cleaned up."

Mason touched her briefly on the cheek, her eyes gazing lovingly on Miranda's face, before she left the bathroom. Miranda looked at herself in the mirror and was shocked to see how pasty she looked. She rinsed out her mouth, wiped her face with a washcloth, and stepped out of the bathroom. Mason and Dennis were speaking quietly in the living room.

"Miranda, can I make you tea or something?" Mason asked, her eyes concerned as she watched Miranda enter the room. She looked exhausted and drained, and Mason wanted to put her arms around her and hold her tightly.

"Nothing right now; I don't think I could keep anything down. I'm sorry for that." Miranda was embarrassed that Mason and Dennis had seen her vulnerability.

"Miranda, don't worry about it."

"I need to explain what I felt and saw just once. Should we go to your office to do that?"

"No, Dennis and I are here and, if it's okay, I'll tape our discussion."

"That's fine." Miranda couldn't look directly at Mason. She needed to be held so badly, but now wasn't the time. She sat on the chair across from her. Dennis sat on the couch, his sympathetic eyes gazing back at Miranda. Mason pulled a portable tape unit out of her pocket.

"This is Detective Mason Riley with Detective Dennis Mayer and civilian Miranda O'Malley. The date is June twenty-first two thousand and three at four twenty-five p.m. We're sitting in Ms. O'Malley's living room after returning from surveillance at Lower Woodland baseball fields. Ms. O'Malley, please begin."

Miranda's eyes closed as she concentrated and slowed down her breathing. She needed to control her emotions to get through this. It took her a few moments to get calm and centered.

"He's already looking for another child and he's going to kill the little girl if we don't stop him. He's enjoying hurting her too much. The images are so horrific, and he is so black inside. He has done this before, and he's not going to stop until he's stolen ten children. That's his number—ten. It has some significance to him. The little girl is still alive because he was thinking of what he was going to do to her next. You must find her. He has her hidden some place very close, and he was gloating about it. He was laughing inside and thinking how no one will find her until he's done with her. It's small and dark and dirty, like a basement, garage, or some other type of shelter, and only one story. This place could be a tool shed. It's very low, and he can barely stand up in it. It's made of wooden slats, and she's handcuffed and laying on a filthy mattress in the corner. She's no longer able to cry but she's still alert. He's playing with her. He likes it when they're scared of him. He's going to keep her alive until he picks his next child, and he's close."

Dennis and Mason watched Miranda as she spoke, enthralled and shocked as she continued. "He's very smart. He knows that we're looking for him, and he knows about the task force. He's confident that no one would suspect a policeman. He's terrified the children into not speaking by threatening to kill their families. He can do it. He has a gun. They'll never be safe from him. He is going to kill. He's done it before, somewhere else with a young woman, and he enjoyed it. What he did to her is beyond belief."

Miranda was unaware that she had been crying the whole time she'd been speaking. She opened her eyes and shuddered, breathing slowly to calm her wildly racing heart. Mason and Dennis remained absolutely silent, neither one sure what to say. They had no doubt that Miranda had connected to the evil man. If her words hadn't convinced them, her terrified face did.

"Dennis, you need to get back to the precinct and start typing your report. I need to go talk to the Chief about what happened. Miranda, can I have your permission to play this tape for him?"

"Yes, of course."

"Dennis, why don't you take off while I finish up here with Miranda?"

"Okay, Mason." Dennis stood up and walked up to Miranda, knelt in front of her, placing his hands gently on top of hers. "Miranda that was one of the bravest and most amazing and terrifying things I have ever seen. You take care, honey, and don't you worry, Mason and I will catch this bastard."

"Thanks, Dennis, I know you will." Miranda smiled back at the detective.

Dennis quickly left the condominium and stepped into the elevator. He was still stunned at what he had witnessed and he had no doubt that Miranda was the real deal. He couldn't wait to tell the others at the station.

Mason stood up slowly and went to Miranda, kneeling in front of her and looking into the wounded eyes of her new lover. Her hand shook as she reached out and stroked Miranda's damp face, her own eyes glistening with tears.

Keeping her voice low, she spoke quietly to Miranda. "You continually amaze me at how brave and strong you are. I will catch him and keep him from harming any more children. You have helped us so much. I want to stay here and hold you all day and night, but I can't, honey."

"Could you just hold me for a minute?"

Miranda's request almost broke Mason's composure. She picked Miranda up and slid behind her to cradle her in her lap. She held Miranda tightly against her, her lips finding Miranda's, more to comfort than inspire passion. Miranda's body softened against Mason's as she wound her arms around Mason's neck and held on. Her body trembled as she gave in to the comfort Mason provided.

"Mason, I need you."

Mason smiled at Miranda's words. "I need you, Miranda. I'm going to need you for a very long time."

Miranda's heart soared at Mason's words. "Can you call me later and tell me what's going on?"

"I'll call you every hour, on one condition—you get yourself into bed and take a nap. You're exhausted, and I need you to take care of yourself."

"I'll lay down for awhile. No matter how late you work, will you come to me?"

"You couldn't keep me away, honey. I'll be here as soon as I can. I'll call if I'm going to be too late."

"Be safe."

Mason kissed Miranda slowly and then hugged her tightly before moving her gently off her lap. She would have loved to stay and comfort Miranda, but she had a job to do and a young girl to locate. "I'll let myself out. Go lie down, honey."

Mason left swiftly while Miranda watched as she disappeared from sight. Miranda felt calmer after being held by Mason; she had felt protected and safe. She stood up still feeling a little shaken and headed for her bedroom. She took a quick shower and climbed into bed. She was fast asleep before Mason had arrived back at her office.

Chapter 17

Mason entered the conference room to find her team hard at work going over Dennis' report as fast as he typed it. Matt turned and looked at her, his eyes full of concern. "How's Miranda?"

"Exhausted and emotionally drained," Mason responded, trying to keep her emotions under control. She wanted to hit something.

"Dennis let us hear the tape before it was transcribed. Mason, it was chilling."

"You should have been there. Let me know what we've got for background on Phil Randolph and Sue March. I need to update the Chief and then we need to go to Sue March's home."

The team quickly got her up to speed and then Miranda dragged her feet down the hall. She dreaded talking to her boss. "Where's the Chief?"

"He's in his office waiting for you."

Mason took a deep breath before she entered. He was more than skeptical of her using Miranda, and the last time they had spoken he had been very angry with her. She had put her job and position on the line with him, insisting on using Miranda. For the first time in her life, Mason could care less about her career. She knew Miranda's information was accurate.

"Chief, have you spoken to Dennis?"

"I did. Is this the tape?" His stern countenance didn't frighten Mason, because she knew that what they had uncovered was the key to solving this crime.

"Yes sir. Before we listen to it, I'll again go on record that I believe Ms. O'Malley's statements to be true and accurate."

"Sit down, Mason. Dennis has already lobbied for you. He also believed her and will rip anyone to shreds if they say different. She must be some kind of woman to make such a strong impression on two of my best detectives. Now, let me listen to the tape and draw my own conclusions."

"Yes sir." Miranda started the tape and sat back in her chair.

The Chief sat motionless until the tape went silent. Mason grew restless in her chair as she listened once again to Miranda's voice. "Jesus, she saw all that?" The tape of Miranda's statement had shaken the Chief.

"I believe so, sir."

"So we have four cars following him?"

"Yes, and two followed the woman home. We've done a complete background check on both of them. I haven't been completely updated on everything yet. Sir, we have no evidence that can be used in court against him, but my gut tells me it's him."

"Then catch him, goddamn it! But check with legal before you do anything. I want this by the book."

"I will, sir."

"And Mason, when this is all over I want to meet this O'Malley woman."

"Yes sir."

Mason hurried out of her boss's office and met again with Matt and Dennis. "What do we know?"

"The woman's background check is clean, but our suspect's is another matter. He has absolutely no record past ten years ago."

"How is that possible?"

"He's using someone else's social security number. He has no history according to the FBI's records and ours."

"How the hell did he become a cop?"

"His police academy record was clean; so were his school transcripts, and he passed the physical and psych exams with flying colors. His time at the academy was stellar. He did extremely well. No one thought to look further back so his lack of records was missed. One nice thing is that we have his fingerprints on file, so if we get a hit on them when we find the little girl, we've got him. The bad thing is we know he's armed and knows how to use a weapon," Matt responded.

"Tell me how in the hell a sick puppy like this gets past a psych evaluation!"

"Beats me, but after we catch him I'm going to find out. Let's go find the little girl. I need to talk to legal before we go. Ben, is the FBI still looking into this guy?"

"Yep; now we have his prints in the system. I'll let you know what we dig up."

"Good; Matt, let's get going. Dennis, I need you to coordinate everything from here. Let me know if this guy starts to move again. As soon as we have anything concrete, we're going to take him down! If you hear anything, call me."

"Will do, Mason."

"And Dennis, nice job."

"Thanks, Mason. If we catch this freak, it's because of Miranda. She's amazing."

"Yes, she is." Mason smiled at the besotted man. And she's mine. Somehow, Mason didn't feel at all petty about gloating over that fact.

"Matt, let's go."

"Mason, I didn't get a chance to listen to all of Miranda's tape. Was she as specific as Dennis said she was?"

"She was. Matt, I can't explain it but she described the place he's hidden the little girl. I know she was right. We're looking for a small storage shed, wooden, with a dirt floor. He's barely able to stand up inside the place."

"Dennis said Miranda knew he'd done this before and that he killed a woman."

"Yes, and he's going to kill this little girl if we don't find her quickly. He's already looking for another child."

"Wow, do you know how she does it?"

"No, but I believe in her."

"So do I. I like Miranda; she's an incredible woman."

"She is. Matt, we don't have any reason to be interviewing the March woman other than her connection to tee ball. She can't know we suspect her boyfriend, otherwise she might warn him."

"Do you think she knows anything?"

"I doubt it. Miranda thought March was genuinely in love with the creep. She might have noticed something important though."

"Can you imagine how she's going to feel when her boyfriend is arrested for torturing the very children she's introduced to him?" Matt's face was full of sadness.

"I can't, and I'm sorry for what we're going to put her through. Her life will never be the same again."

"Jeez, that's just so damn sad."

Chapter 18

"She hasn't left the house since we followed her here. The other unit's been parked in the back alley behind the garage," the plain clothed detective reported to Matt and Mason. He and his partner were parked a discreet distance down the tree-lined street.

"Good. You both stay out here. Let me know if our perp makes a move. I don't want him to surprise us while we're talking to her. Matt and I are going to meet with her right now." Mason and Matt climbed the front stairs, knocked and waited impatiently for the young woman to open the front door. She opened the door with a pleasant smile that was immediately replaced by a look of surprise when Mason held her badge up.

"Ma'am, my name is Detective Riley and this is Detective Gains. We're from the Seattle Police Department and would like to talk to you about a missing child. May we come in?"

"Of course. Why do you want to talk to me?"

"A connection has been made with the missing child and your tee ball league, and we need to see if you've noticed anything suspicious. Our records show that you coach a team."

"Yes, that's right. I've been a coach for three years. Please, have a seat. I'm surprised my boyfriend didn't ask me about this. He's Officer Phil Randolph. He's also a Seattle policeman. He's been very concerned about the missing child."

"We all have. It's bothered us very much. Can you tell me whether you've noticed any young, single, clean-cut men hanging around the park?"

"Not one that I didn't know. I wish Phil were here. He's much more attentive to details than I am. He knows all the kids' names, who their parents are, and where they live. He helps me almost every weekend when he doesn't have to work."

"He sounds like an observant man."

"He is. He loves kids so much, and he's so good to me. He not only helps me coach, he's helping me remodel my house so we can both live in it together." She sounded so happy that it made Mason's chest hurt. She was going to be destroyed if her boyfriend turned out to be the man they were hunting.

"So he doesn't live here?"

"No, he has an apartment in Redmond, but he's here almost all the time. He's taken over the garage for his workshop and banned me from it. He does all the woodworking in it. Do you want me to call him? He's coming over here tonight. We're going out to dinner and a movie."

"No, you don't need to call him. If we need to talk to him, we'll get in touch with him while he's on shift." Mason smiled at the unsuspecting woman.

"You know, I've always wanted a wood shop. I love working with wood. Do you think Phil would mind if you show me what his setup is like? Maybe I can convince my wife to let me have one." Matt smiled engagingly at Sue. No one could resist Matt when he turned on the charm.

"Sure. I haven't been in the garage for several months so I don't know what to expect." Sue led the way through her stylish, small home and out into a tiny, well-landscaped backyard. There was a detached garage next to the alley and connected to the south side of it was a small storage shed about the size of a bathroom.

Mason's heart raced as she glanced over at Matt to see if had noticed the shed. He had. His strides increased in length and his eyes hardened the closer he got to the garage. Sue fumbled with the door and was surprised to see it locked, a large padlock securing the entrance.

"I didn't know Phil locked the garage, and I don't have a key." She seemed puzzled to find it locked up tight. "I'm sorry, detectives. I didn't know it was locked."

"That's okay. I'll just take a look in the window." Matt moved over to the one window, peered in, and was surprised to see his own face reflected in the glass that was covered on the inside with blackout material. Mason had surreptitiously moved around to where the shed was connected to the garage. She was dismayed to see no entrance to it from the outside. The only entrance into the shed was from inside the garage. The small building matched Miranda's description exactly, with its slatted wood walls. Mason started to move back around to where Matt and the woman stood when a spot of color caught the corner of her eye. A bit of red was visible stuck under the wall of the shed, and she bent over and pulled on it. Stuffed under the corner of the plank wall was a filthy, red tennis shoe, small enough to fit a young child. She knew that tennis shoe by heart. Her missing little girl had been wearing ones just like that when she had been taken. Mason felt the adrenalin pump through her body as she turned and spoke to Matt.

"Matt, call for backup and an ambulance." Mason pulled her gun out of her shoulder holster as she approached the locked door. "Ma'am, I want you to step back, please."

"Backup needed in the rear of the yard; all units in the neighborhood respond. Call for an ambulance immediately!" Matt requested as his gun appeared in his hand.

"What are you going to do?" The young woman had no idea why the woman detective had pulled out her gun and was pointing it at the padlock hanging on the garage.

"Matt, hold her while I blow this lock off." Mason quickly fired into the doorway, breaking the wood around the hasp until she could push her way through the doorway. The two plain-clothes officers appeared with their guns drawn just as Mason shoved the door in. While one of the officers ushered Sue out of the way, Matt joined Mason as they pushed their way into the dark garage. Three other officers surrounded the building.

"Matt, try and locate a light in here."

Both Matt and Mason fumbled around in the dark until Matt located a wall switch and flipped the lights on. The garage was set up as a woodworking room with a table saw, drill press, and other pieces of equipment. The garage was flooded with light now, and the locked door to the attached shed was glaringly obvious. New hinges and a padlock gleamed in the bright lights.

"We need something to pry the door open. I don't dare fire my weapon."

"We can pop the pins out of the hinges with this hammer and screw driver," Matt responded as he glanced at Mason. They both prayed that the little girl was in there and alive.

The two worked in silence. Years of partnering made talk unnecessary. Their breathing was labored as they struggled to get to what they both believed was a very terrified and hurting little girl. It seemed to take them forever to get the pins out. The final pin fell to the floor, and Matt and Mason stared at each other for a brief second before pulling the door ajar enough for one of them to squeeze through. It was pitch black in the shed.

"Mason, you go first. She won't be as scared of a woman."

Neither detective wanted to believe the little girl was no longer alive. Mason turned to Matt with an anxious look, and Matt grasped her hand and squeezed in support before she stepped into the room, her weapon in front of her. Her eyes quickly grew accustomed to the dark and she noticed a filthy mattress stuffed in the corner, a pile of what looked like rags lying on the top of it. She moved closer and bent over to search it. She steeled her heart before pulling the rags back hoping against all odds that the little girl was alive. Two terror-filled eyes stared back at Mason, as the child cringed away and prepared for some new pain. Her face was streaked with dirt and gaunt with hunger and fear. Mason dropped to her knees and laid her gun on the ground as she uncovered the naked little girl.

"Matt, she's alive. We found April." Mason's voice broke with emotion as she slowly moved closer to the little girl, trying not to frighten her any more. "You're going to be okay, honey. Everything is going to be okay."

Mason didn't touch the little girl for fear of scaring her, but as soon as the little girl saw Mason, she threw herself into her arms and began to sob. Mason cradled the little girl to her and whispered softly, telling her that she was safe. Mason's face was streaked with tears as she rocked her gently, wishing she could erase everything that had happened to the child. Mason stood up slowly and backed out of the shed as Matt wedged the door open so she and the little girl could squeeze through. Matt watched as Mason moved slowly around the equipment.

"Guys, back up away from the garage so Mason can get her out without frightening her." Matt followed behind Mason, his eyes as full of emotion as Mason's. "Mason, I've got your gun."

"Thanks, Matt."

"Who is that little girl, and what is she doing in my shed?" Sue kept her voice low, her face full of shock and disbelief. As she saw more of the little girl in Mason's arms, she drew back in alarm. The evidence of the little girl's abuse was obvious—dried blood on her thighs, bruising on her arms and legs. "What happened to her?"

"Ma'am, we need you to come with us, please." The detective took Sue by the arm. "We need to ask you some questions."

While Matt and the other detective began to call in the crime scene investigators and support, Mason whispered softly to the mute little girl while they waited for the medical personnel to arrive. The word had gone back to the precinct that they had found the missing child. Mason could see how the little girl had suffered, but she was alive and would be returned to her parents where she belonged. At long last they knew who the man was that had been terrorizing her. It was only a matter of time before they arrested him and put him away. "You'll be okay, honey. Your mom and dad have been looking for you. They'll be so glad to see you." The little girl's arms were locked around Mason's neck and nothing could have pried her loose. "Matt, have you called the precinct?"

"Yes, and he's still in his apartment. The Chief called April's parents and they're going to meet us at the hospital."

Mason's tear-filled eyes met Matt's and she smiled. He returned the smile, both glad they had found the tiny victim but extremely disturbed by her condition. "Good. Nice job, partner."

"You too, but I think we need to thank Miranda."

"Call her, please? And have a car bring her to the hospital. I would like the parents to know who found their little girl. I'm sure they'll want to meet her."

"I will. The other units will continue to shadow our suspect until we tell them to do differently."

"Tell them to pick him up now and bring him in for questioning," Mason responded, her voice full of authority. They needed to get this guy in custody immediately.

"Will do. I wish I was the one picking him up."

Mason looked up at Matt and wasn't surprised to see a look of violence on his face. Matt might be a loving, gentle man but he also had a darker side. Having been his partner for a long time, Mason had seen this side of Matt, and she respected it. He was someone who kept his temper under tight control, but now it was simmering just beneath the surface. She had the same problem. When they ran into disturbing criminals, they had to work doubly hard not to turn into vigilantes, meting out their own brand of judgment. It was a line they had never crossed, but at times like this it was very difficult not to.

Mason heard the ambulance pulling up in front of the house, and she began to move slowly across the yard. Within minutes, Mason was sequestered in the ambulance with the little girl while Matt followed them in her car. The child refused to let go of Mason, and the paramedics hoped she would be less frightened once she saw her parents. They were not going to do anything to scare her at this point. They completed a cursory check of her vitals, and she was stable. Both medics had been moved by the obvious signs of torture on the little girl's body. Mason covered her with blankets and held her as securely as possible. Finally, the ambulance pulled up to the Harborview Hospital emergency entrance.

Matt met them as the doors of the ambulance opened. "The parents are inside with the Chief, Mason."

Mason walked quickly through the emergency room doors and saw the faces of the waiting parents. Tears of joy and relief ran unchecked down both of their faces as they caught sight of their little girl. "Baby, its Mommy and Daddy."

The little girl's face lit up, and she smiled as her mother pulled her into her arms. Her husband wrapped both of his arms around the two of them. He couldn't speak, he was so overcome with emotion. He cried unashamedly while holding tightly to his wife and daughter.

Mason stepped away from them and turned to Matt, her eyes filled with tears. Matt was not unmoved, though he tried to appear stoic. "Jesus, Mason, we found her."

Mason reached up and hugged the overwrought man. "Miranda found her."

"Yes, she did, and we need to arrest this fuck and put him away for good."

"We will, Matt." Mason hugged him once more and turned to her boss who stood waiting for his detective to fill him in.

"Nice job, detectives."

"We aren't done. Miranda O'Malley should get the credit for finding the little girl."

"She will."

"We need to go get the suspect in custody."

"You will. The crime scene investigators are going over the shed and garage, but I have some new information. Your suspect's fingerprints got a hit with missing children in New Hampshire. Ten children went missing a little over six years ago; all were found two to three weeks after being horribly abused. The suspect left his fingerprints in the home of a missing child. They never located him."

"How did he get by his fingerprint search when he became a police officer?"

"His prints from New Hampshire weren't in the system yet."

"Well, we've got him now."

"Chief, Detective Riley, the news service found out our suspect's name and announced it! They also reported that a psychic named Miranda O'Malley helped find the child," an officer informed them as he approached.

"Shit, he's going to run! Someone escort Miranda to the hospital; the media is going to attack her!"

"Mason, Miranda is already here. She's okay. The parents are talking to her right now." Matt tried to calm Mason. It was unlike her to overreact this way.

Mason's eyes darted about until they found Miranda being hugged by the father of the little girl. The mother was refusing to relinquish the child to anyone. The emergency doctors and nurses stood by, waiting to examine the little girl, but they could wait until the mother and child were ready. Miranda stepped away from the father, her face full of tears as he thanked her. She felt Mason's eyes on her and she looked up. The smile that she bestowed on Mason shook Mason's composure to the core as she stared at the beautiful woman she now loved beyond life. All Mason wanted to do was to take her home and love her. Her feelings were so much more than just love. She knew she wanted a lifetime with Miranda—a lifetime and more.

"Detective Riley." A police officer stepped up and spoke to her and Matt, but Mason didn't hear a word he said as she continued to gaze at Miranda, her attention riveted on her stunning face.

"Mason, Mason!" Matt finally got her attention. "We lost him."

"What?"

"We lost him. The detectives surrounding his apartment building went to arrest him. He wasn't there. They searched the whole building and the surrounding area. He was gone. There's an APB out on him and there are units continuing to look."

"Shit, shit, shit!" Mason was royally pissed.

"Mason, what's going on?" Miranda approached the angry woman.

"He got away. The freak got away."

"I'm sorry." Miranda was as dismayed as Mason. "He isn't done, Mason. He's going to find a way to complete his cycle. Until he gets to the number ten, it's incomplete."

"Do you think he'll relocate?"

"No, I think he'll stay here and change his looks. He may have another safe place to hide out in. His girlfriend may shed some clues." Miranda placed her hand on both Matt and Mason's arms. "I'm sorry you didn't get to arrest him, but you found April."

"Miranda, *you* found the little girl. We should be celebrating." Mason turned to her and smiled. Miranda's touch on her arm had a soothing effect, and she needed that physical connection with her. "April is going to be okay."

"Yes, she is, because of detectives like you and Matt."

"Thanks Miranda, but I think you deserve all the credit." Matt blushed with embarrassment. "Mason, the Chief would like to meet Miranda."

The Chief of Police stood next to Mason, watching the threesome. "Miranda, this is my boss, Chief Marston. Chief, this is Miranda O'Malley."

"Hello, Ms. O'Malley. I have to admit I wasn't at all enthused when Mason brought you in on the case." The look on the man's face was mixed with humor and relief. A mischievous smile played on his lips.

"I can understand that." Miranda grinned up at the burly man.

Mason chuckled as she watched Miranda charm the socks off her boss. "So you're a psychic."

"Rumor has it." Miranda's expression was full of humor.

"You don't look like a psychic." Mason had to agree with her boss. Miranda was wearing a mint green dress and matching jacket, high heels completing the look. Her hair was full of soft curls and loose down to the middle of her back. She looked professional, smart, and incredibly sexy.

"You don't look like a cop," Miranda responded, as she looked at the overweight man in the professionally tailored three-piece suit.

"That's what my wife says." Chief Marston patted his stomach as he chuckled. "In all seriousness, I want to thank you for helping my detectives find the little girl."

"I did very little. Your detectives did all the work."

"You're very charming. I can understand why my best detective was willing to put her job on the line to keep you on the case."

Mason blushed as Miranda turned to look at her, her face incredulous. She turned back to the Chief. "She put her job on the line?"

"She was willing to put her Detective's shield on the line to keep you working on the case. I was a little bit skeptical about using your talents."

"So you thought I was a whack job too?" Miranda teased him as she caught the expression on Mason's red face.

"A whack job—that sounds like my favorite detective. See, we were both wrong."

"Chief, the mayor is on the line for you."

"Excuse me; I'm going to have to take this call. Miranda, thanks again for all your help. And I hope our narrow minded police department hasn't discouraged you from working with us again."

"Chief, if I can ever be of any help, your detectives know where to find me." Miranda shook the man's hand, smiling the whole time.

"Mason, I expect a full report within the hour in my office."

"You'll have it."

"I like him," Miranda commented, as he walked away, a cell phone pressed to his ear.

"He likes you."

Miranda turned to face Mason. "You put your job on the line to keep me on the case."

"It sounds worse than it was. I knew you were right about what you had seen."

"Mason, we have to get back to the precinct. Dennis is interviewing the girlfriend."

"Okay, Matt." Mason turned to Miranda, an apology in her eyes.

"What time are you done tonight?"

"Pretty late, I would guess."

Miranda smiled and whispered softly so that only Mason could hear, "I'll be waiting."

Mason grinned in response. "I'm sending you home with a police unit, and I want the officer to stay with you until I get there."

"There's no need for that."

"Miranda, just do it, please?" Mason's eyes were soft with affection and love.

Miranda acquiesced with a nod. Mason quickly made the arrangements and, as she and Matt headed for their car, she watched Miranda safely escorted to the police unit and on her way home.

Chapter 19

▼

"Dennis, what have we got?"

"She doesn't know much and right now she's in complete shock. There is a possibility that he has access to a cabin somewhere. He's been promising to take her there. I have the FBI looking for any property that might be in his name. We've got his driver's license number and the social security number he's been using. His bank account hasn't been touched. We've got a trace on his cell phone and his truck's been impounded. He's just up and disappeared."

"Miranda believes he's going to remain in the area and change his appearance. He may have another girlfriend that he can go to. She thinks he won't leave until he hits the number ten. He'd have a plan in place for something like this. He probably had another vehicle stashed along with some cash."

"Mason! You have a call—it's him!"

Mason followed the excited detective out of the conference room, Matt and Dennis beside her. "Is someone notifying trace?"

"Yes." Another detective handed her the telephone.

"Hello, this is Detective Riley."

"Hello, Detective, do you like my game?" Mason remained silent waiting for him to continue. "I didn't expect to run into such a smart cop here in Seattle. It's made the game so much more fun. And to bring in a psychic—that was brilliant, if I do say so myself." His voice was confident, arrogant and made Mason's skin crawl.

"What do you want?"

"I want to play with you, detective. I'm going to turn up the heat, and I hope you're able to stand it. By the way, that psychic is a beautiful woman. She'd be such fun to play with. I could do so many things with her."

The line went dead in Mason's hand, but she was too shocked to move. "Did we get him?"

"No, he didn't stay on long enough."

"Matt, he's going to go after Miranda!" Mason's face registered the terror she felt. "He's going after her! I've got to call her!"

"Mason, you put an officer inside her home. Call the officer, while I send another unit to watch from outside."

Mason quickly got the officer on her radio. "Officer Martin, you're to stay with Ms. O'Malley until I get there and do not leave her side. She's in imminent danger. Do you understand? You tell Ms. O'Malley that I'll call her and explain what's going on."

"Yes, ma'am."

"Dennis, keep trying to locate that cabin. He has to have a hiding spot somewhere."

"Will do, Mason."

"Matt, what did the crime scene investigators get from the garage?"

"Everything. When we catch him, he's going away. There was evidence of all three children being in the shed. He's going down, Mason."

"We just have to catch him, damn it!" Mason and Matt strode back into the conference room. Mason picked up her cell phone and dialed Miranda's number.

"Hello?"

"Miranda, it's Mason."

"Mason, what's going on?"

"He called me and he hasn't left, just as you thought. He still wants to play his game."

"He's escalating, he won't stop at kidnapping."

"Miranda, he's transferred his attentions to you." Miranda remained silent waiting for Mason to continue to speak and then it dawned on Mason. She had known he would. "You aren't surprised! You knew he would!"

"I wasn't completely sure until now."

"I don't want you to go anywhere. Stay in your condo with Officer Martin. We have another unit outside and I'll get there as soon as I can."

"I'll be fine, Mason."

"I know, because I won't let anything happen to you. Miranda, I..."

"Mason, I'll be fine; do your job, honey." Miranda hung up the telephone.

"Is she okay?" Matt asked concern in his voice.

"She knew she would end up as his target."

"Jesus, Mason! Why didn't she say something?"

"She said it hadn't been clear until now."

"We need to get busy. I'm going to go over Dennis' interview notes."

"Good, I have to go update the Chief after I pull everything together. I'm going to check with the lab and then Ben to see what the Feds have come up with. Then I'm going to Miranda's."

"You're going to stay there for the night?"

"Yes. Matt, I need to tell you something," Mason lowered her voice and looked up at the man she trusted completely. "Miranda and I were together last night."

"You…and her?" Matt was almost at a loss for words.

"I think I'm in love with her." Mason's stating it out loud made it very real.

Matt's look of shock, then pleasure, relieved Mason's worried mind. "Oh, wow, Jena isn't going to believe this—you and a psychic!"

"A gorgeous, sexy psychic."

"Well, yeah, but Mason, you called her a whack job." Matt's chest rumbled with laughter.

"She forgave me." Mason grinned.

Matt hugged her tightly. "I'm glad for you."

"Thanks, Matt. The whole thing's been a total surprise, and I'm still not sure how it's all going to play out."

"How does Miranda feel?"

"I think she feels the same way."

"Good, I like her." Matt grinned. "Boy, is Dennis going to be disappointed."

"She's mine," Mason announced proudly.

Matt's face grew serious, as he thought of Miranda being the target of the maniac they were trying desperately to catch. "Mason, we need to keep Miranda safe. He can't know you and Miranda are seeing each other. That will make her even more important to him."

"I know, Matt; God, I know. I'm going to go over there and stay tonight but I'll leave officers outside for the night and we'll have her under twenty-four hour protection."

"Do you want me to stay with you?"

"No thanks, Matt. You go home to your wife."

"Mason, I'm very glad for you."

"Thanks, Matt."

It was after ten before Mason was able to get away from the office and leave for Miranda's. She had spoken to her several times and called as she pulled up in front to let the officers and Miranda know she had arrived. After a briefing with the two men outside, Mason rode up on the elevator and approached Miranda's door. She knocked, and the woman officer opened the door slowly, checking the hall behind Mason.

"Hello, Officer Martin; how is everything?" Mason entered the darkened condo.

"Fine, ma'am. Ms. O'Malley is in her bedroom, and I've checked all the windows and doors several times."

"Good, you head back to the station and clock out. I'll take the next shift."

"Detective Riley, I'm really glad you found the little girl."

"I didn't find her, Ms. O'Malley did."

"Is April going to be okay?"

"Given time, she will be."

"Good, I'll see you tomorrow. Goodnight."

Miranda had quietly entered the living room, wearing a nightgown and matching robe. She had known the minute Mason arrived. "Good night, officer."

"Goodnight, Ms. O'Malley." The young woman left the condo.

"She wants to be a detective just like you. She worships you," Miranda commented as her eyes traveled over Mason's tired face.

"Everyone wants to be a detective." Mason shrugged it off as she set down her overnight bag and turned to Miranda. "I'm so sorry that you have to put up with this."

"Mason, I could put up with just about anything to have you here." Miranda smiled as she slid her arms around Mason's neck and gently held her. "Kiss me, please."

Mason wound her arms around Miranda and bent to meet her lips. It was a soft, loving kiss that caused a slow-moving warmth to radiate through both women's bodies. Mason's tongue probed Miranda's mouth as she felt passion surge through her. Over and over they kissed until Miranda was trembling in Mason's arms.

"I've never wanted anyone as much as I want you. You fill every part of my body with need until I feel like I'll melt."

"I feel the same way, Miranda. I told Matt about us tonight."

Miranda pulled away from Mason and looked up in to her eyes. "Was he okay with everything?"

"He's happy for us."

Miranda's smile was huge as she looked up at Mason. "So detective, do you think you could follow me into the other room? I have plans for us."

Mason grinned as Miranda tugged on her hand. Snatching up her overnight bag, she allowed Miranda to pull her into the bedroom. Within moments the two women were naked on the bed. Mason's hunger to touch Miranda was almost as ferocious as Miranda's need to love Mason. They drove each other higher and farther until the waiting became too much. Mason's hips were sealed against Miranda's, and Miranda's arms held Mason tightly against her body. Slowly, Mason rolled her hips as their throbbing centers touched intimately. It was the perfect joining of two women's bodies. They moved harder and faster until Miranda's cry of pleasure drove Mason over the edge. Moaning loudly, they held their fused hips together as they trembled, eyes open and locked on each other. Mason arched her back to increase the pressure, as Miranda's fingertips slid across her cheek. Tears of pleasure glistened on Mason's face as she bent down and kissed Miranda before collapsing on top of her.

For a long time the two women lay clutched in each other's arms unwilling to let go of the moment. Miranda's gentle hands stroked Mason's strong back and shoulders. Mason's face lay buried against Miranda's neck.

"I could stay like this all night," Mason admitted as her fingers played in Miranda's long hair.

"So could I. I just want to go to sleep with you on top of me," Miranda responded, her heart still pounding in her chest.

But Mason wasn't quite finished. Her hand snaked down and quickly entered Miranda's wet, sensitive center, driving her into another orgasm. "Oh my, Mason."

Mason stroked Miranda deeply, her skillful fingers filling her completely. Miranda turned her face into Mason's, wanting Mason's mouth on hers. As they kissed, Mason's tongue mimicked the stroking of her fingers and drove Miranda crazy until she dissolved once again with pleasure so acute she began to cry.

"Now, I can go to sleep," Mason whispered against her mouth, before kissing her once again. "I want to be inside you when you fall asleep." Miranda melted with emotion once more.

Not to be outdone, Miranda slid her hand between them and cupped Mason's dripping center. She wasted no time entering her and holding her fingers deep inside her while Mason's body throbbed around them. Mason threw back her head and groaned and then once again slumped onto Miranda's body.

"Now, we can both go to sleep."

The two women drifted quickly into slumber, still locked together. Even in sleep they did not move apart.

Chapter 20

Miranda couldn't stop smiling the whole time she worked in her office. She was in love, completely and totally in love. It had been a week since she and Mason had been together for the first time. They had spent every single night together since that first night. Neither one wanted to spend a night apart; their feelings grew stronger and more passionate with each passing day.

Mason and her team were still working long hours trying to locate Phil Randolph before he kidnapped another child. They weren't even sure he was still in the area. They had gone over and over the information that they had collected trying to locate a single shred of evidence that could help locate him. They repeatedly reviewed everything, hoping against hope that they would find the lead that would allow them to catch him before he harmed another child.

"Ma'am, I know you're exhausted; we just need to go over these files one more time."

"Detective, if I knew anything I would tell you. I've given you everything from my home—all my bills, my telephone records, my clothing. I don't know anything more."

Matt's gentle eyes stared at the young woman whose life had been turned inside out in a matter of a week. No amount of counseling would ever erase the disgust and horror that Sue felt when she was reminded she had been in love with a killer. The fact that he had left her bed to torture and abuse children he had hidden in her garage had made her physically ill. A psychologist that Miranda had recommended to help her begin to deal with her terror was treating her. She had not physically returned to her home but was living with her parents who guarded her fiercely. "Sue, I know you're trying to help us. I just need you to think of every conversation you ever had with Phil. Did he ever mention that he liked to do something like hike or camp or fish?"

Sue's gaunt eyes stared at Matt as she tried to recall anything in her memory. "I already told you he liked to spend time in the mountains camping at some cabin."

"Did he ever mention where?"

"No, I just know he would go away for the weekend sometimes to camp."

"Did you get the impression that it was far away?"

Sue sighed as she watched Mason enter the room. She knew Mason quite well. Mason had spent many hours interviewing Sue with compassion and understanding. Sue was as much a victim as were the children Phil had preyed on. Mason understood how much heartbreak Sue was dealing with and appreciated the fact that Sue was still willing to help. She had volunteered to continue with the hours of interviews, even though they were taking a physical toll on her.

"Sue, you need to go home and get some rest. I'm going to have an officer take you home."

"I'm okay, detective."

"You're exhausted and need to get some sleep."

"One more hour."

"Sue..."

"One more hour."

Mason smiled at the brave woman and placed her hand on her arm. "I have a suggestion that Miranda made and I want to try it, if you're willing. I'm going to say a word and you say the first thing that pops into your head."

Sue looked at Mason with a ghost of a smile and nodded her head in the affirmative. "Okay."

"Date."

"Dinner."

"Romance."

"Candles."

"Weekend."

"Cabin."

"Mountains."

"Snoqualmie."

"Camping."

"Snoqualmie." Sue shook her head as she remembered. "He stays at a cabin up at Snoqualmie Pass. That's where he goes. I remember now, he mentioned once that he would take me there for a weekend."

"Good, Sue. Can you remember any details?"

"It doesn't have electricity or running water because he mentioned he had to carry in wood and water. He also couldn't drive to it; he had to hike in. I remember him saying that it was hidden from the road." Sue had become excited as she began to remember a little more. "He purchased a generator to take up there—a diesel generator."

"How long ago?"

"A couple of months ago. He took it up three weeks ago on a Sunday and went there and back in one day."

Matt and Mason finally had something to go on. "What time did he leave in the morning?"

"Not too early, around nine, and he was back at my house by five."

"Great, Sue. Matt and I are going to go start identifying known cabins around Snoqualmie. You're going home to get some rest."

"Mason, I have to help." Sue's eyes filled with tears as she spoke. She needed to do everything she could to help catch Phil. As long as he was loose she wouldn't be able to rest. It was her fault that she hadn't stopped him from hurting the children. She should have seen the signs. It was her fault that they hadn't caught him by now. She would do anything to make up for her failure. She should have seen something, done anything to stop him.

Mason understood what Sue was going through. No matter what anyone said to her, Sue would always blame herself for not recognizing the monster in Phil. She needed to help put him away. Her need was the only thing keeping her sane. "Okay, Sue. Matt, can you get Ben and the others to come to the conference room? I'm going to talk to the Chief."

"I will. Come on, Sue, let's get you a cup of tea."

By the time Mason joined the rest of them in the conference room, the wall was partially covered with an aerial map of the Cascades. Ben was on the computer and Dennis was on the telephone. Sue and Matt were putting pins in the map while others attaching notes in various places. Mason had been gone a little over an hour, but obviously a lot of work had already been done.

"The owner of this one is a woman who works on Mercer Island as a real estate broker. It fits Sue's description. You have to hike in to it."

"That makes fourteen cabins we've identified so far. There have to be others we're missing."

"He wouldn't choose a cabin that would be easily found. He wants privacy. He'd pick an isolated place where he'd feel safe."

"He'd own it or lease it. Where's that list of aliases he's used? We need to run every known permutation through the system." Sue was no longer being interviewed. Her quick mind and desperate need to help had turned her into a member of the team.

Four hours later, they had found the cabin and were preparing to send in a SWAT team. He had leased a cabin under the name of someone who had died years earlier. They knew it was Phil; the cabin met all of his requirements. All warrants had been issued, all the paperwork was in order, and Sue had been sent home with an officer after Mason promised to keep her posted about ongoing events.

Mason and her team split up and stepped into the waiting FBI helicopters. Within minutes they were airborne, silent and anxious as they anticipated the job ahead of them. The SWAT team was being transported in two military helicopters already on their way. Forty-five minutes later, Mason watched as SWAT surrounded the small cabin and prepared to enter.

The structure sat in a small clearing surrounded by dense woods. No one would have stumbled on the cabin if they hadn't been looking for it. Even during the day it was well hidden by the old growth forest surrounding it. There were no signs of movement as the well-trained SWAT team lobbed a smoke grenade through the window and broke through the door.

Ten minutes later the all-clear sign was given, and Matt and Mason were allowed to enter the uninhabited cabin. What they saw filled them both with sick terror. Every wall was covered with pictures of terrorized and tortured children. This was his den of iniquity. He had documented in living color every sick thing he had done to each child.

"Jesus, I think I'm going to be sick," Matt admitted, as he took deep breaths trying to keep the bile from rising in his throat.

"Matt." Mason spoke barely loud enough to be heard.

Matt turned and was stopped cold. One wall was dedicated to Miranda. Hundreds of pictures covered the space from floor to ceiling. There were pictures of Miranda at work and in her home. He had been stalking her!

"We need to get to Miranda, now!"

"Mason, she's being guarded twenty-four hours a day."

"Tell me how the hell he took these pictures?" Mason was enraged. There was one shot of Miranda undressing in her bedroom.

"He has to have wired her condo."

"Matt, he could be anywhere." Mason looked up at her partner, her face streaked with tears.

"We'll go now. The rest of the team can work the scene. We'll go, Mason."

Miranda had absolutely no clue what they had discovered. She was happily catching up on her office files, having sent Colleen home after their last appointment. She was so content with her life that even the prospect of catching up on her piles of patient files couldn't alter her good mood. She was going to put in another hour and then head home. She and Mason were going to have a romantic dinner and watch a sappy movie that Miranda had picked out. Mason had grumbled and made a face, but she had acquiesced. She would do anything to make Miranda happy. Miranda was startled by the police officer entering her private office. They usually waited for her in her reception room.

"Officer, do you need something?" Miranda felt a little bit of fear creep in as the officer turned to face her. Miranda's face turned stark white as she looked into the dead eyes of Phil Randolph.

"I need you, Miranda." He showed her the gun in his hand. "You helped the cops and stole my toys from me. Did you think I would forget you?"

"How did you get in here?"

"It was easy once I put the idiot in your front office out of commission."

Miranda could only stare up in shock as she realized he was going to kill her too. His thoughts emanated from him in black waves of thick, oily evil. He was going to hurt her before he killed her. The plan was already in his mind. He walked slowly up to her, the gun pointed at the middle of her chest. He was in full police uniform, and he was alone with her. "I was one of many people who helped to find you. They know who you are."

"Of course they do—at least who I am today." He was too arrogant. He knew he was going to get away with the abduction.

"They're going to catch you." Miranda needed to keep him talking.

"I imagine, eventually, but not before I've had my little bit of fun." He smiled disarmingly at Miranda, and a shiver ran down her spine. He was pure evil and he was standing in her private office. She was terrified.

"Matt, he's going after Miranda. I need to call her and warn her."

Matt took Mason's hand as she dialed her cell phone. He was as terrified as she was. Miranda was startled when her telephone rang. It was her personal line, and she knew it was Mason.

"Don't answer that telephone."

"I'm expecting a telephone call. If I don't answer it they'll know something's wrong."

"If you make one wrong statement, I'll shoot you where you sit." Miranda knew he meant it. He would enjoy killing her.

"Hello."

"Miranda, it's Mason."

"Hello, Detective Riley. How's the case coming?"

"Miranda, what the hell…" Mason stopped talking and took a deep breath. "He's there."

"Yes, Detective, I can help you tomorrow, just let me know what time."

"We're on our way."

"Good, I'll be there." Miranda settled her mind and sent as many of her thoughts as she could to Mason. She had to rely on their strong connection and Mason's skills. Mason would save her.

"I love you," Mason whispered.

"I feel the same way." Miranda hung up the telephone.

"So your girlfriend is calling you to warn you. She won't get here in time. We'll be long gone before she gets here. Now, I need you to get up out of your chair and come with me. I'm going to have this gun at your back as we go down the rear stairway. If you try to get anyone's attention, I'll shoot you and anyone else that tries to interfere. You'll be responsible for their deaths."

Miranda moved quickly, fearful of the possibility of putting someone else's life in jeopardy. She stumbled getting to her feet, and she felt his evil eyes watching her as she moved to the center of the room. Her whole body reacted as she felt his sickness inside her.

"You don't know how much you messed up my plans. It was going to take me all summer to play with my ten little toys, and you screwed it all up. I might even have married that bitch, Sue. She was interesting, especially when I left her bed to play with my toys. She never even suspected me, that is, until the cops told her. I owe you for that, and I'm going to make you pay." Phil stood in front of her, his face frozen in a cold smile.

Miranda stood without moving, watching the man talk to her. She could feel her skin crawling with fear. She couldn't outrun him or his gun. She couldn't think of anything to do but stall and hope that Mason would arrive soon. "I don't understand why you hurt children."

"Because I can." The statement was so arrogant it shocked Miranda. This was not a man, but a monster, and she couldn't forget that. She needed to focus and read his thoughts without letting him know she was doing it. Her life depended upon it. She slowed her breathing down and probed lightly into his mind preparing herself for the horrifying images he might be picturing. Flickering scenes flashed in her mind as she focused on his face and kept her emotions from him. It took all of her efforts to keep herself from shaking or crying as she viewed what was in his fractured mind.

Chapter 21

▼

"Jesus, Matt, can we move any faster?" Mason was ready to throw herself out of the helicopter as they hovered over the roof of Miranda's office building. Miranda's office was on Eighth Avenue in a twenty story high-rise with roof access. She and Matt had called for help from SWAT and two other police teams with the stipulation that they stay outside the building until Mason and Matt had gone inside. They had to know what was going on before they stormed the building.

Matt jumped first and Mason followed him, rolling to her feet and racing with him into the building. Their counterparts had already connected with the security guard sitting at the front desk. He had camera access to every floor.

"Where is he?" Matt whispered into the radio as he and Mason entered the stairwell and tore down the stairs. They were on the tenth floor and Miranda's office was on the fourth floor.

"He's coming out of Ms. O'Malley's office into the reception area. He has a gun pressed to her back."

Mason swore as she heard the comment over her headset. Her heart froze in her chest. She had to save Miranda; she just had to. "Matt, we need to get ahead of him. He won't go out the front door; he'll use the parking garage."

"If we take the elevator we might beat him down. I don't think he would take the elevator."

"Jack, can you see the elevators?"

"Yes."

"Is he heading for the elevator?"

"No, he's heading for the north stairwell."

"Do you have cameras in the stairwell?"

"Yes, and he's forcing Ms. O'Malley to go downstairs."

"Can you control the elevators?"

"Yes, I have control of them from here."

"Can you express us straight down to the parking garage from the eighth floor, first elevator?"

"Yes."

"Do it!"

Mason and Matt threw themselves into the open elevator and hit the down button. Neither spoke as they watched the floors shoot by. They needed a break, just a few minutes to get into position in the underground parking garage. "Where are they now?"

"Still going down the north stairs. He's going slowly and watching both above and below. Your elevator is going to open in the parking garage. You'll be about twenty feet from the stairwell."

"Can they get out any other way?"

"Only if they come out through the lobby."

"SWAT, we've entered the parking garage. Surround the outside entrance, and when we say so, we want you to enter through the front lobby and close off the stairwells."

"Will do, Detective."

"Matt, I'm going to take a position behind this car. Can you get a clear shot of him from behind that pillar if I get his attention?"

"I don't know, Mason." Matt tried to keep anxiety from his voice. Miranda's life depended upon how he and Mason performed.

"They're coming to the door." The voice crackled over the com line.

Mason and Matt took their positions. The door slowly opened, and the two detectives watched Miranda and then the man dressed as a police officer come into view. Mason almost cried out when she saw Miranda held tightly against Phil's body, the gun now pressed into her upper chest. He wasn't taking any chances. If Mason couldn't get him to point the gun away from her, Miranda's life was dangerously compromised.

"I think you and I are going to have to go somewhere where I can take my time getting to know you. You're going to stay right next to me until we get to my truck. I'll kill you if you move even one inch away from me." Phil's lips slid against Miranda's face as he growled in her ear. Then his tongue darted out and slid across her neck. Mason watched in fury as she saw him tighten his grip on Miranda. Her stomach recoiled in hatred when she saw him lick Miranda's neck.

Miranda struggled to stay focused. There was so much emotion swirling around her. Phil's absolute evilness—his obsession to kill—was bombarding her with images. His thoughts were very clear to Miranda. He was going to take her to a deserted cabin, someplace up in the mountains, and take his time killing her. She could see it so clearly, and she had no way to stop him. He was planning to torture her until he killed her, and Miranda was sick to her stomach. She had to do something, anything, to get away from him.

Phil's mouth moved against her ear as he spoke to her while they moved slowly in the direction of a dirty pickup truck. "You smell terrific. It's too bad you know who I am. We could have dated awhile, and I could have continued to play with my toys and fucked you at the same time."

Miranda tried to concentrate, but fear leached through her body and made her tremble. She began praying that Mason was on her way. She couldn't think of any other option. She had to slow him down to give Mason time to get there.

"Mason, you need to stop him now. He's fifteen feet from a truck. I think it's his."

"I'll try and get Miranda's attention." Mason frantically began to think about what to do. She prayed that Miranda knew she was there.

"Mason, you're betting her life on her ability to read you."

"It's all we have, Matt." Mason concentrated and began to send her thoughts to Mason. Over and over she spoke to her in her mind.

Miranda felt something push away Phil's violent thoughts, and she concentrated on trying to make it come into view. It was Mason, and she was telling Miranda she was there and very near. She wanted Miranda to stop moving and stumble. She needed Miranda to fall all the way to the ground, giving Mason the opportunity to get a shot at Phil. It was a huge gamble, but Miranda knew if he got her in his truck, she would die. Holding her breath, Miranda prepared herself and then slumped heavily down to the garage floor, catching Phil by surprise.

He still had a grip on Miranda's arm as she went limp and lay prone on the cement floor of the parking garage. He bent to drag her up against him, the gun for a brief moment pointed away from Miranda's body. There was the sound of gunfire, a flash of light. Miranda squeezed her eyes shut and was aware of the pounding of feet on the pavement around her head. She lay numb on the ground, her eyes shut, shaking with terror.

"Miranda, Miranda, honey, are you okay? Sweetie, talk to me. Are you okay? God, please be okay." Mason was unaware that tears ran freely down her face as she tried to rouse Miranda. Meanwhile, Matt handcuffed the bleeding, now sullen former police officer. Mason had winged his gun arm causing him to release his hold on his revolver. As the gun fell from his hand, Matt had tackled him from behind before he could pick up his gun and get a shot off.

"Mason, are you injured?" Miranda sat up and ran her hands over Mason's face and arms, panicked that Phil had hurt her. Her hands shook as they passed over Mason's body.

"No, I'm not hurt, honey. Are you okay?" Mason's eyes were wild with worry, her heart still pounding in her chest.

"I've got a couple of skinned knees and elbows, but I'm fine." Miranda was also crying. She couldn't believe that they had both survived.

"God, I'm so glad. Jesus, I thought he was going to kill you!" Mason lost it as she hugged Miranda to her, shaking with fright, her face streaked with tears. Mason couldn't keep from crying, her heart overflowing with emotion.

"Mason, we're both okay. It's okay, honey, everything is okay." Miranda held tightly to Mason as they both tried to regain their composure.

"Mason, SWAT and the backup units are waiting to take over the scene, and a medic unit is here." Matt stood over the prisoner, his gun trained on him, but he managed to smile at the two women who still sat on the dirty, oil covered parking garage floor, their arms tightly wrapped around each other.

Mason wiped her face clean of tears and stood up, holstering her gun before helping Miranda to her feet. The prisoner remained completely silent, as he lay flat on the ground, his arm bleeding profusely. SWAT personnel and several police officers stood in groups just inside the parking garage grinning as they waited for the all-clear from Mason. They were relieved that they had gotten to Miranda in time and that they had captured the maniac that thought torturing a child was a game.

"Guys, come on in. Matt has him all trussed up." Mason grinned back at the crowd of officers. "Matt, you did real good taking him down."

"I did great, and so did you. Nice shot, partner. I sure am glad you and Miranda are on the same wavelength." Matt's grin was wide, his dimples winking in his cheeks.

"So am I, Matt, 'cause I'm going to live with her for the rest of my life."

Matt's look of surprise and pleasure was almost as special to Mason as was the look of delight and love she saw on Miranda's face. Mason couldn't believe she had just proposed to her in front of a dozen police officers. Not a very romantic setting in which to commit herself to Miranda.

"I think we have a lot to talk about tonight," Miranda commented with a big smile.

"Yes, we do." Mason grinned as the paramedics approached them. "Do you mind my announcing it to Matt and the rest of the world?"

"Not at all; I told my mother and grandmother a week ago," Miranda admitted with a laugh. "But I think the SWAT team might have a little fun teasing you about your outburst."

Mason flashed her trademark smile at Miranda before turning to greet the SWAT team and her backup unit. She didn't care who had heard her. Then she once again became the professional detective that Miranda had fallen in love with, and Miranda's heart filled with love and respect for the woman who had saved her life.

"Okay guys, let's load up this piece of trash and haul him away," Mason announced, as she watched the medics begin to work on the prisoner. A second medic began cleaning up Miranda's knees and elbows.

Matt and Mason waited until the handcuffed prisoner was loaded onto a gurney and, accompanied by two police officers, was lifted into the ambulance and taken away. Miranda refused to go with the medics to the hospital, and she sat quietly out of the way in a police car, while Mason and Matt took care of the remaining details. The door to the car opened and Miranda jumped reflexively before she realized it was Chief Marston.

"Ms. O'Malley, I'm sorry to startle you, especially after all you've been through." The Chief kept his voice gentle smiling at the woman who had been through such a nerve-wracking ordeal.

"That's all right." Miranda's heart all but pounded out of her chest. It would be a long time before she recovered from being a victimized by a madman. "I'm fine, Chief."

"I just wanted to check on you and make sure that you're being taken care of."

"I am. To be honest with you, I'm enjoying the peace and quiet." Miranda smiled up at the large man. She was having a hard time trying to keep everyone's thoughts at bay. When she was stressed or extremely tired, she found it difficult to keep her shields up to avoid being pummeled with people's feelings and thoughts. "I have to thank you for having such well-trained police officers. They saved my life."

"I understand that Mason was able to communicate with you mentally. I have to tell you I don't understand it, but I'm indebted to you for all your help with this case. I believe you are very talented."

"I'm glad I could help, and I'm extremely grateful that your detectives got here in time."

"I don't think Mason would have let anything stand in her way." The Chief's eyes twinkled. His lead detective would have walked through a steel wall to save Miranda. Their relationship had not gone unnoticed by the Chief. He, for one, was hoping that Mason had found someone with whom to share her life. All good cops needed a healthy relationship to support them. "We need to get you out of here."

"I believe Matt and Mason are sending me home with two officers."

"I'll go check on their plans. I'm certainly glad you're okay."

"So am I, Chief Marston. So am I."

Chapter 22

"Matt, I'm out of here. Go home."

"I will, Mason. Before you go, can I talk to you?"

"Sure." Mason worried a little bit that Matt was somehow bothered by her relationship with Miranda. Everyone in the department knew about Miranda and Mason. The detectives hadn't let her get two feet in the door before they started teasing her about her romantic proposal.

"Hey, Mason, you sure are suave when it comes to proposing."

"Bite me, Ken."

"You've got great timing. You could take out an ad in the paper."

"Shut up." Mason took the ribbing with an indulgent smile on her face. She didn't care what they said to her, but Matt was her partner, and his feelings meant almost as much to her as Miranda's.

"I have to tell you, Mason, I was scared today," Matt admitted as he stood next to his partner.

"I was too."

"I don't know if I could ever do what you did today if my wife had been in Miranda's place."

"Of course you could. You'd always do your job and protect every last person as if he or she were precious to you. It's what we do."

"I can't believe with all this going on that you and Miranda had time to fall in love." He poked his partner. "I didn't even know you liked her."

"I don't know how it happened, but I'm going to be thanking God for a long time for keeping Miranda safe." Mason stood up and hugged Matt tightly. "I don't know about you, partner, but you have a wife to go home to, and I have someone who means more to me than my own life. I'm going to Miranda, and I'm going to hold on as tight as I can all night, just to remind myself that she's okay."

"Mason, I'm very happy for you." Matt's red-rimmed eyes glistened with unshed tears.

"Thanks, Matt. You're my dearest friend and I love you."

Matt's eyes overflowed as he gazed down at his best friend. So much had happened in the last week, and all of their emotions were high. "I love you. C'mon partner, let's get out of here."

The two detectives headed out of the deserted task force conference room and entered the detectives' bullpen. A round of applause greeted them, along with a few hoots and cheers.

"Nice going, Matt."

"Great job, Mason."

"Excellent work."

Their friends and fellow detectives congratulated them as they made their way to the door. "Mason, Matt, a minute of your time," the Chief bellowed through the open door of his office.

"Yes, sir."

"How are you both doing?"

"Fine, sir."

"Mason, the shoot looks fine, and internal affairs is going to put it in writing. I should have your weapon back to you in day or so."

"Good, sir."

"I don't want to see either one of you in the office until next week. Take four days' paid leave."

"But…"

"No buts; I don't want to see either of you in the office until next week."

"Thanks, Chief."

"You're both welcome. Nice job today. And Mason, tell Miranda I'm very glad that she's okay."

"I will, Chief."

"Now, go on and get out of here." The satisfied look on the Chief's face was reassuring to both detectives. He was proud of his unit, and they respected him very much.

They hurried out of his office with gratified smiles on their faces. "Hey, Mason, it looks like the Chief knows about you and Miranda."

"I don't care who knows. Last one to the parking lot is a rotten egg." Mason bolted for the stairs, a grinning Matt in hot pursuit.

Chapter 23

After the paramedics had checked her one last time. Miranda had been driven back to her condominium by two police officers. One officer sat outside the condo while a female officer sat in her living room waiting for Mason to arrive. Mason had threatened the woman officer with her life if she left before then. Miranda had thought it would be hard to be alone in her condominium after what had just happened, but she actually felt safe and calm. She loved her home and was hoping that Mason would love it also, because she was going to ask her to live with her.

"Officer, I'm going to grab a shower. Before I do, is there anything I can get for you? Something to drink—juice, water, coffee?"

"No, I'm fine; thanks, ma'am."

"I'll be out shortly."

"I've already checked all the doors and windows as Detective Reilly asked. Everything is locked up tight."

"Thank you, officer, I appreciate that." Miranda didn't feel unsafe anymore, especially since she had her own personal bodyguard to watch over her. She knew Mason would always take care of her, as she would take care of Mason.

Miranda scrubbed her body clean and washed her hair. Her scrapes stung a little, but not too badly. She wanted to scrub every trace of that man's touch from her body. She had just finished drying her hair when she heard voices from the living room. Mason was talking quietly to the officer, but Miranda had known the minute she arrived. She and Mason were very closely connected and extremely sensitive to each other. She entered the living room just in time to see Mason ushering the officer out the door. "Mason."

Mason turned and faced Miranda and sighed deeply. "You are so unbelievably beautiful."

"I love you." Miranda's voice was soft and full of love.

Mason closed the distance between Miranda and herself and picked Miranda up in her arms. "I love you, and I will love you for the rest of my life."

Their lips met in a kiss, slow, full, a promise made, as they renewed their feelings for one another. Mason held Miranda tightly to her as she walked them into the bedroom. She needed to see for herself that Miranda was unharmed, and she could think of no better way than to make love to her. "I thought he was going to kill you, and I was so scared. I've been scared before, but nothing like what I felt when I saw him holding the gun against you."

"You spoke to me in your head. You sent your thoughts to me and I could hear you clearly."

"I knew you would hear me, I just knew it." Mason's face was inches from Miranda's as they spoke.

"You trusted my capabilities and you saved my life." Miranda reached up and placed her hand against Mason's cheek.

"You trusted me to save your life." Mason began to cry.

Miranda stood next to the bed enclosed within Mason's arms, smiling up at the comely woman who had given her the only gift she needed in her life. All that Miranda had ever wanted was trust from a woman who loved her. And she had found it in a tall, beautiful detective, who had looked at her and, in one moment, fallen in love with her.

Mason began to cry deep heavy sobs, as Miranda tightened her hold on her. "Everything is okay, honey."

"I was so scared. It would have killed me if he had hurt you."

"He didn't baby, and you saved me."

"I love you so much." Mason buried her face against Miranda's neck.

"I need you to love me, Mason."

"I do love you."

"I mean physically love me, so that I can forget what that man wanted to do to me." Miranda's eyes were vulnerable, her heart open.

"Are you sure?" Mason didn't want to rush Miranda. She had already been through so much.

"Mason, read my mind," Miranda whispered as she looked into Mason's beautiful, expressive eyes.

Mason looked down into Miranda's stunning face and smiled at her. "You do love me."

Miranda laughed as Mason rolled her gently onto the bed, kissing her until she was breathless. Mason proceeded to make love with Miranda long into the night until both of them were exhausted. The stress of the last crazy week had taken a toll, and they grew sleepy. They had renewed themselves with beautiful, physical lovemaking.

"Miranda, did you really tell your mother you loved me?" Mason asked as she sleepily stroked Miranda's back.

"Yes, and she's coming to visit with my grandmother. She'll want to meet you."

"Where are they going to stay?"

"Here with us."

"What do you mean with us?"

Miranda was just on the verge of falling asleep. "Would you move in here with me? I want to live with you, Mason. I don't want to waste any time we have together. I want to be with you for the rest of our lives. I want to grow old with you."

"What about your mother and grandmother?" Mason watched Miranda's face carefully; this was so important.

"They'll love you."

"Miranda, I would love to live with you. How soon can you make room for me?" Mason grinned at her lover.

"Tomorrow."

"Good, because I have a week off, and I can move really fast."

"I love you, Mason. From the first moment we met my heart recognized you."

"Miranda, I love you. From that first moment, you and I were destined to be together. Can you go to sleep?"

"I can as long as you're holding me."

"All night long, honey, and for the rest of your life."

Chapter 24

▼

"Grandma, this is Mason Riley. Mason, this is my grandmother, Rose Donnell, and my mother, Moira O'Malley."

"Hello, Mrs. O'Malley, Mrs. Donnell."

"Heaven sakes, call me Rose. How'd you get the name Mason?" Miranda smirked as Mason's eyebrows rose in surprise. Rose couldn't have been bigger than a minute but she was certainly not shy. Her short, silver hair curled around her intriguing face. She moved quickly, and her eyes were full of humor and curiosity.

Miranda grinned widely as she watched her grandmother match wills with Mason. Miranda knew that Mason was going to be able to hold her own with her grandmother. They were two peas in a pod. Since Mason had moved in with her, Miranda had realized that the serious police detective was only one side of Mason. She was playful, funny, and stubborn as hell, just like her grandmother.

Miranda's mother, Moira, slipped her arm around her daughter and hugged her. "I think Mama has met her match," she chuckled as she watched Mason and her mother. It was apparent that Mason was not going to be a pushover.

"I know she has," Miranda laughed. "She and Mason are going to be trouble, you just wait."

Miranda's mother hugged her daughter playfully. "You look very happy, honey."

"Mom, I am so happy, I can't tell you how perfect my life is. Mason loves me." Miranda's eyes filled with tears as she shared her happiness with her mother.

"It's about time you found someone who knows how special you are."

"She knows, Mom. She trusted me to read her thoughts and she saved my life."

The look of wonder and love on her daughter's face thrilled Miranda's mother. "I'm going to want you to explain everything to me in great detail, but first your grandmother and I could use a drink. I think we could all use one."

Miranda headed into the kitchen to get them all a glass of wine. Mason followed her. "Can I help with dinner or anything?" she asked, coming up behind Miranda and hugging her.

"You can kiss me, than carry these two glasses of wine out for Mom and Grandma."

"I like your mom and grandma."

"I knew you would."

"I wasn't worried about liking them. I am worried about them liking me."

While the two young women were whispering in the kitchen, Moira and her mother were having a similar discussion in the living room.

"What do you think, Mama?" Miranda's mother asked her mother.

"I think Miranda has found her partner and soul mate. I like her. She's honest, charming, and scared to death we aren't going to like her."

"Then we'd better make sure she knows we do."

"Hell no! I'm going to make her work for it," her mother responded gleefully.

"Mama!" Her daughter shot her a warning glance.

"I can't make it too easy on her; that's my granddaughter she's living with." Rose grinned, her eyes full of mischief.

"Mama, I love you." Moira kissed her mother and squeezed her tightly. There was no one like Rose Donnell.

"I love you, too. Now, where is Mason? I still haven't learned why she was named Mason."

Mason grinned at Rose as she came out of the kitchen. The woman's attitude tickled her. "I was named after my grandfather on my mother's side. He was a police officer in Detroit for many years."

"Was your father a police officer?"

"No, he was an office supply salesman." Mason's father wouldn't have understood her passion for becoming a police officer, but she thought her grandfather would have. He had made it to the rank of detective before he retired. While she was growing up, she had peppered her mother with questions and asked for as much information as she could get about her grandfather's occupation. Mason had wanted to become a cop since she was a little girl.

"It must be pretty exciting running around cracking cases."

"I like it." Mason smiled at the inquisitive woman.

"Have you ever shot anyone?"

"Grandmother," Miranda reprimanded her with a long look.

Undaunted, Rose continued. "So, can I see your badge and gun?"

"Certainly; they're in my bedroom." Mason turned and walked down the hallway, the diminutive woman in her wake.

"Can I shoot your gun?" She asked as she trailed after her granddaughter's new lover.

"Not in your wildest dreams," Mason responded with a snort, as Miranda and her mother grimaced at the remark.

Rose was unfazed as she continued to pepper Mason with questions. "How often have you fired your gun? Have you ever killed anyone? Do you know karate?"

While the two women discussed guns and badges in the bedroom, Miranda and her mother visited quietly in the living room. "Honey, are you sure you're okay?"

"Mom, I'm fine. In fact, my life is wonderful. I have to pinch myself just to make sure it's real." Miranda's eyes once again filled with happy tears as she smiled at her mother. "I never thought I would find this kind of relationship. Mason is so incredible. She accepts me for who I am. My being a psychic doesn't bother her at all. She even teases me about it."

Moira smiled at her besotted daughter. "She does?"

"She told me we shouldn't have any fights since I already know what she's thinking, and I can do everything she wants before she has to ask." Miranda's laugh was full of joy. "She even calls me to ask me what numbers to pick in the lottery and then says, 'Never mind; that wouldn't be half as much fun'."

"She sounds like a sweetheart, honey. I'm glad you found each other."

"Mom, it's so important that she loves me for who I am."

"Yes, it is, and I'm so happy for you, honey."

"Thanks, Mom."

"Do you think Mason is going to fold under Mama's badgering?"

"Not a chance!" Miranda laughed heartily.

Chapter 25

▼

"I can't believe you took Grandma to the police academy!" Miranda laughed as she crawled under the covers next to Mason.

"It's the only place I felt safe around your grandmother and guns," Mason confessed. "In case you haven't noticed, she's a little obsessed about firearms right now."

"You made her day! She was so excited that they gave her a SWAT jacket."

"Hey, your grandmother could have talked them out of anything. They all loved her. She's game for anything. You should have seen her at the gun range. She put one dead center in the bull's-eye. She's a natural!"

"God, don't tell me she's convinced you to get her a gun."

"Are you kidding? Your grandmother and a gun—I'm not crazy." Miranda could hear the affection and pride in Mason's voice.

"She's your grandmother, too."

Mason's eyes filled with tears as emotion flooded through her body. She leaned over and kissed Miranda slowly, a kiss full of love and feeling. Miranda sighed as Mason's lips whispered over her face with gentle, loving kisses.

"I love you, Miranda."

"I love you, honey."

"I love your mom and grandmother."

"I know you do, and they love you."

"I just feel so damn lucky." Mason's voice trembled with emotion. She had a family, a real honest-to-God family.

"How about you get even luckier when I make love with you?"

"With your mother and grandmother in the room next door? I don't think so." Mason looked panicked as she stared back at Miranda.

"Honey, they're staying with us for two weeks," Miranda whispered, her fingers sliding over Mason's flat, muscular stomach.

"But what if they hear us?" Mason moaned as Miranda's fingers slid between her legs.

"Mason, honey, I need to love you."

Mason had no defenses against Miranda's lips and hands, and Miranda knew just how to please her. She quickly aroused Mason's body with her attentions. First Mason and then Miranda were tossed into orgasms that shook their bodies and filled their hearts with love. Despite their attempts to be quiet, Miranda's mother and grandmother could hear the sounds of their lovemaking through the walls of their bedroom.

"It sounds to me like my granddaughter has found a lover that curls her toes," Rose whispered to her daughter.

Miranda's mother chuckled softly. "I've always hoped she would fall in love."

"Maybe now you can tell your daughter about Armand."

"Mama!" Moira wasn't surprised Rose knew about her lover. Rose knew everything.

"Well, daughter, don't you think I know when my only daughter is having good sex?"

"Great sex."

"Hah, it's about time," Rose snorted as she pulled the covers up to her chin.

"Mama, I'll tell Miranda when I'm good and ready to."

"She needs to know."

"That her mother is sleeping with a man?"

"That her mother is alive, healthy, and deserving of a life. I know you loved Joseph, and losing him so early broke your heart. But, I would love to see *your* toes curled by a lover."

"Mama, Armand curls my toes," Miranda's mother snickered in the dark.

"I need a lover. I'm the only one not having great sex. Maybe the gardener would be interested?"

Miranda's mother giggled. "He's twenty-six, Mama."

"Good, he'll have a lot of energy and be able to keep up with me."

Mason and Miranda heard the laughter coming from the other bedroom and they smiled as they snuggled against one another.

"Sounds like your mom and grandma are having a good time."

"They always have a good time."

"You're all so close."

"Being different makes us all a little closer."

"You and your mom could be sisters, you look so much alike. You're both beautiful."

"She is beautiful. She's sleeping with a very nice Creole gentleman named Armand."

"She told you?"

"No, Grandma did."

"Does it bother you?"

"Not at all; I like him very much. I hope she marries him."

"Miranda, would you marry me?"

"I'd love to. You really would want to marry me?"

"More than anything I wish we could get married, and maybe we will one day." Mason cuddled with her and smiled. "That leaves just your grandmother."

"Don't you put it past her! She's always looking for a boyfriend."

"Maybe I'll take her back to the police academy. There are a lot of young studs hanging around." Mason grinned as she wrapped her arms around Miranda.

Miranda dissolved into laughter. "My grandmother with a cop! Heaven forbid."

Mason and Miranda burst into more giggles as they settled against one another.

"Love you." The two women drifted into sleep—happy, contented, love-filled sleep.

They were four women—one family—full of affection, love, and wisdom. Three were gifted women and the fourth loved all three unconditionally. Wise women. Wise love.

The End

978-0-595-39018-2
0-595-39018-8

Made in the USA
Monee, IL
22 April 2022